"I've been in love with you since we met," Kitty said

She leaned toward Bolan, her eyes closed, her lips slightly open.

Bolan raised his brows, shifted closer and caught the motion of her right hand. It darted to her open-necked blouse faster than he thought possible and came away with a three-inch blade.

She jammed it toward his chest, thrusting forward with all her weight behind it.

The Executioner's one brief glimpse of her snaking hand gave him time to move and roll off the log.

But the woman lunged at him, the knife tracking for his heart.

MACK BOLAN

The Executioner

DON PENDLETON's EXECUTIONER

MACK BOLAN

Orbiting Omega

A GOLD EAGLE BOOK FROM

TORONTO • NEW YORK • LONDON • PARIS
AMSTERDAM • STOCKHOLM • HAMBURG
ATHENS • MILAN • TOKYO • SYDNEY

First edition June 1984

ISBN 0-373-61066-1

Special thanks and acknowledgment to
Chet Cunningham for his contributions to this work.

Printed in Canada

Technology does not improve the quality of life; it improves the quantity of things. Improving the quality of life requires the application of wisdom.

— *Neil A. Armstrong*

There can be no respect for a cause that seeks its victory through the suffering of innocents. And there can be no dignity for a ''warrior'' who seeks the easy prey of unarmed civilians.

— *Mack Bolan*

In recognition of all those experiencing
the rigors of basic training.
Hang in there!

1

A 5-round burst of screaming lead hornets turned the darkly silent Arizona landscape into a hostile environment. Mack Bolan executed a face-down dive to a rocky ledge.

The Executioner scowled. No one knew he was coming up here tonight. He had left his vehicle two miles back and walked in, moving so silently that not even the horned toads and night-crawling tarantulas had enough warning to scurry out of his way.

But even with all his precautions, someone knew he was here.

In the quarter-moon dimness Bolan stared at the surrounding harsh, dry land. He was in the low country southwest of Phoenix, in an area called the Sand Tank Mountains. As he stood and began to move, five more chattering rounds whined over his head. He recognized the snapping sound of an M-16's output: 5.56mm sizzlers.

No one could see him there in the gloom. No one could have heard him walk in. Yet the automatic fire was aimed within a few feet of his location.

That could only mean they were using electronic vibration sensors, an electric warning fence. He hit the ground again and crawled ahead, feeling around for a small rock. He found one and threw it ten yards to his right. Before the stone stopped rolling, a burst of automatic-rifle fire peppered the air above the area where he had pitched the rock.

The blistering M-16 rounds did not hit the ground. They were firing high. Bolan reasoned that the sensors had detected the intrusion and warned someone above. So now, up there on top of the little mesa, they knew for sure an intruder was approaching. That would make it more interesting.

At least the defenders didn't have infrared spotting scopes, which would have taken away the dark, making him visible. He was thankful for one small advantage.

Bolan crouched, then stood, moving toward the access route that he had selected just before dusk by using a twenty-power scope. If he had to climb to the top of the mesa, this was the best way and evidently the most heavily defended.

The Executioner continued forward softly over the rocky soil to reduce the vibrations his boots transmitted to the ground. If he walked lightly enough the sensors would not be able to track him. His stealth lasted two minutes, then his foot slipped and kicked free a rock that tumbled down the slope. Bolan crouched low.

A rattle of automatic-rifle fire came from above and this time from more than one position. Three different sensors must have picked up the path of the rock as it rolled downward. Bolan looked above and could see the winking muzzle-flashes.

Damn fast reaction time. They must have professionals on top. Bolan wondered how many men would be defending the strongpoint? A dozen, maybe twenty?

The odds did not bother him. The Executioner usually worked alone and almost always against big odds. He was ready and back in action.

Five minutes later he was at the cleft, a twenty-yard-long stretch of boulders that formed a natural passage from the shelf he was on to the next higher one. It also was in a direct line of sight from the top of the mesa. That could be fatal.

At least he had not triggered any more sensors. Mack Bolan had no desire to close out his Executioner's career on this Arizona wasteland, cut down by some chance round fired blindly in the middle of the night.

A diversion—that was what he needed.

Bolan unhooked two grenades from his webbing, and when he was at the start of the access route, he threw the small bombs as far to the left as he could. When the second one was still in the air, Bolan ran around the first boulder, along what looked surprisingly like a trail up the slot.

The grenades exploded and brought three responses from the automatic rifles to the left. Then a new deeper sound came, as single-round rifle slugs splattered lead on the rocks ten yards to his right, whining into the distance. Seven of the rounds boiled in near him, after Bolan slid behind a protective granite slab to wait out the fusillade.

When the last shot faded, he left the safe position and moved upward cautiously. His immediate goal was to get to the top of the mesa wall and secure the facility before dawn. With daylight there might be Air Force, NASA and Army assault troops coming in from all directions, dropping in by chopper and probably ruining any evidence left up there.

Bolan also hoped to surprise any defenders or stragglers acting as rear guards and get some vital information from them. He had not counted on a stubborn defense like this from what must surely be only a temporary location.

Now it seemed he would have his share of a firefight

before he got to the top. The Executioner was prepared. He carried a fully automatic Ingram Model 10 submachine gun on a cord around his neck. Across his back was slung a Childers experimental battle automatic shotgun with a specially shortened barrel.

The Childers was only eighteen inches long overall, had a forward-curving, 20-round magazine for 12-gauge ammo. A slightly rear-slanting front-mounted grip gave a firm second handhold on the automatic shotgun pounder.

This weapon was so new it was still a prototype, but it had worked extremely well for Bolan in tests. He had it loaded with double-ought buck rounds. It could fire single shot or full automatic. It had a forward-moving barrel and fixed breech block, and empty rounds exited to the rear of the magazine.

Over his battle-black skinsuit Bolan wore combat webbing that held two remaining grenades and a lightweight Colt Commander .45. A K-Bar fighting knife and a dozen other small combat surprises completed his arsenal. The Executioner did not have a long gun on this mission. He would not need one.

He moved silently, slower, but with more respect for the early-warning system they had planted. He deduced it was not just a "fence" but must be an interconnected series of rings and panels. That sort of a warning setup was difficult to devise and expensive to install.

The existence of this facility proved that this was not a nickel-and-dime operation. Any outfit that could electronically steal an orbiting communications satellite and then viciously kick it out of orbit so it dropped into the atmosphere and streaked across the U.S. sky in prime viewing time as a twenty-million-dollar blazing comet, must have big-money backing. He still had not figured all the angles to explain why anyone would deliberately ruin such valuable and expensive hardware and disrupt worldwide communications.

Bolan worried about his next move toward the summit. The mesa he was climbing was not high or spectacular. But what was on top was the important part.

To his right he saw the forty-foot-wide "grand highway" that sloped gradually the last two hundred feet to the crest. It was too easy. And he was sure it would be staked with sensors and might be mined as well, presenting a perfect concentration point for massed enemy fire.

Instead, Bolan went for his next choice, straight up the crumbling sides of the forty-degree slope just ahead. It would be a two-hundred-foot climb to what had looked through the scope like a temporary rock wall around the rimrock of the mesa.

He had estimated that the flat area on the summit was less than an acre in size. But enough electronic equipment had been flown in there to capture and destroy the communications satellite.

Bolan threw a rock upward onto the broad open path and listened as an automatic rifle fired from above and scrambled the air across the slope with a firestorm of sizzlers. Again he could see the flashes from the hidden guns. The rounds went high.

Bolan moved faster, more deliberately. Any trip wires along here could be fatal—they would be invisible in the darkness. Touching a wire with his foot might trigger a flare, a grenade or a deadly antipersonnel mine.

He had seen enough of all of them in Nam for a lifetime.

The Arizona night was strangely quiet. Bolan wondered what the defenders were doing, thinking. He had not attempted to confuse them by a series of probes. He was moving straight up the hill to do battle.

So far he held a minor strategic advantage: he had not fired a shot. To do so would give away his exact position, and the defenders could concentrate fire on that spot rather than wait for a sensor reaction.

Bolan reached behind his back and loosened the battle shotgun so he could swing it around for immediate action. He had never seen a handheld weapon chew up targets the way the Childers had. Amazing.

Bolan felt a wire on his right boot, but by the time he jerked his foot back he heard the wire snap and the instantaneous sharp crack of a small charge.

The Executioner rammed himself against the rocks, waiting for the explosion. Five seconds later he lifted his head and heard a familiar "pop" high overhead. Flare.

He froze, holding one hand over his closed eyes, but even so he could see the brilliant white light that blossomed from the parachute flare as it burned with blinding intensity, snapping his formerly wide-open pupils into pinpoints, reducing his vision to zero.

When the deadly, twenty-second burn was over and he could no longer see the light through his fingers, Bolan opened his eyes and let them adjust to the darkness again.

Noise. That was the problem. There was no battle noise, nothing to indicate an attack, no men's voices, no confused talk, yells back and forth or any commands being barked. It was not like any battle Bolan had ever been in.

Either the men on top were seasoned veterans or they were combat virgins and so frightened they were afraid to talk. That worried him. Either group would be particularly dangerous in a fight.

Bolan's vision reverted to normal and he made a run up the slope, not worrying about the noise factor now. He was under the lip of a small overhang that would be hard to fire at from the wall. He scrambled upward, clawing at the rocks, pulling himself up now hand over hand.

When he was ten feet short of the top of the wall, he stopped. Again there was utter silence, not even a night-bird's call or a coyote's howl, only the gentle sighing of the Arizona desert night wind around the rimrock.

Bolan shifted his forward movement twenty feet to the left, where the slope was more gradual and the wall on top appeared to be slightly lower. He pulled up the Ingram, held it in his right hand and put the fire-selector lever on full automatic, then he ran for the wall.

Curiously, this time there was no challenging fire. They should have had a string of final warning sensors along here. He was five feet from the top of the wall and breathing hard. Then another two steps and he thrust one hand over the parapet. With a jump he heaved his body to the top of the rock jumble and rolled over, his finger still on the submachine gun's trigger, his eyes searching for danger, targets.

Nothing.

In the gloom he could see no one.

There was no sound of human activity around the top of the parapet.

He stood and ran along the wall. Twenty feet down he came to a gun mount, carefully set up with sandbags. It was an M-16 with a drum magazine that held seventy-six rounds. All sandbagged in and ready to fire.

Bolan frowned as he lowered the Ingram. A weapon ready but no gunner. The men must have pulled out on command.

The Executioner quickly circled the hilltop fort. There was no one anywhere, no human defenders were on top of the desert tableland.

Now he saw a shack in the center. It was a prefab unit, portable and new looking, not desert-sun weathered. Bolan ran to it on a zigzag course but drew no fire. He tested a door, found it unlocked and pushed it inward. It swung open on oiled hinges.

From inside came the hushed throb of a sound-proofed diesel engine. Bolan struck a match and held it high. He saw a diesel engine running a generator. A bank of batteries sat to one side and beside them, blinking in the sudden light, a foot-long Gila monster. He was urging the lizard out the door when he noticed a light bulb with a pull-chain switch overhead before his match burned out.

He jerked the switch downward and light flooded the interior of the shed. Now he would make a closer inspection. A workbench on one side held a breadboard device filled with wires and electronic gear. The breadboard had dozens of sets of complicated switches and relays, which were all connected on one side to a black box that had an antenna leading out a small window. To the other side was another black box that held more switches, relays and other electronic gear.

Bolan shook his head as he contemplated the display before him.

In a flash he realized what it all meant. It could not be! But it was.

Bolan ran outside and picked a heavy rock beside the closest mounted M-16. He saw that the weapon was anchored firmly in place. He also noted that the gun had some special equipment and two wires leading from it into the dust at his feet.

The Executioner tossed the rock over the side. He heard it rolling downhill. Just beyond the first shelf the rock bounced and kept going. Something clicked beside him and at once the M-16 chattered off a 5-round burst.

Bolan snorted in frustration. He had put in a dozen hours planning and sneaking up on an empty fortress, one that was undefended except by electronic sensors and radio-relay-triggered weapons.

It was a complex setup, but would be simple for the electronic genius involved here. The sensors planted below were tiny broadcasting sets that picked up vibrations, broadcast the intrusion to the radio in the shack, which sent a message by wire to the closest weapon, firing it by remote control.

Not a single human defender was needed on the whole blasted mesa. Something else bothered Bolan. He had been fired at, but missed. Even on the broad highway area the rounds had been high over a man's head. Another irony. The person who designed this little setup had built in another safeguard. No matter how many troops stormed up the mountain, and no matter how careless or poorly trained they were, the automatic fire had been carefully aimed so not a single round could possibly harm any attacker.

Sound and fury with a purpose. But what was the purpose?

Bolan hurried back to the shack and searched it. At first he found nothing important. It had been systematically stripped of all identifying marks and papers.

He checked his watch: 0330 hours, another two and a half hours until dawn, when the reported assault teams would arrive by land and chopper. They would probably probe first with land troops, then attempt a helicopter strike.

Bolan searched the shack again, inch by inch. Half an hour later he found near the door a scrap of paper wedged into the floorboards. There were numerals on it, some kind of a rubber stamp impression and a series of four words. He pocketed the slip of paper and kept looking.

Bolan took the cover off the black box and found serial and model numbers that he copied in a small notebook from a slot pocket in his skinsuit. Next he went outside and wrote down the serial numbers from three of the M-16s. Finally he looked under each sandbag holding down the weapons. He replaced the bags exactly as they had been. He wanted to keep the surprise intact for the Army and NASA people.

On the next to last of the twelve gun mounts, he found a matchbook cover under one of the sandbags. It was from the Stag and Stallion bar in Winslow, Arizona. Bolan pocketed the cover. His search was ended.

The Executioner vaulted the low wall and walked down the slope away from the mesa. He had a two-mile trek back to his rented vehicle. He went through the sensors and heard the automatic weapons firing from above and knew the rounds were at least twenty feet over his head.

Bolan wished he had time to wait to see how NASA and the assault troops fared against the mock defenders. There would be a lot of red military faces. But he had less than an hour to get out of this area and back to the public highway before he met any of the ground troops that he was certain would come in by truck.

Mack Bolan was moving again, on his own, not directed or instructed by anyone, answerable to no man. And he wouldn't quit until he found out the reason for the twenty-million-dollar prank, until he located the perpetrators and made sure that such a theft did not endanger the U.S. space program.

2

As Bolan drove toward the highway he sent a silent message of thanks to Aaron "The Bear" Kurtzman back at Stony Man Farm. Kurtzman was still there, paralyzed from the waist down by KGB assassins when they had shot up the farm trying to kill Colonel John Phoenix. But Kurtzman had survived, confined to a wheelchair, with the Stony Man Farm computers his sole responsibility.

Now he had developed into Mack Bolan's one secret link with the Farm and the vital and vast storehouse of information in the largest computer data banks and linkups in the world. As in the past Kurtzman could learn almost anything through the Farm's links with government and private data banks. He was Bolan's mole at the farm.

Bolan contacted him from time to time, and once in a while Kurtzman had something to pass on to Bolan. It was all highly irregular and unofficial. No one else at the Farm knew of the contact.

The Executioner admitted that he missed his people, his teams. Able Team and Phoenix Force were still functioning from a rebuilt Stony Man Farm. They were good men, and he wished them well. But that was another life, another time.

When Kurtzman wanted to contact Bolan he had no way of knowing where the Executioner might be, so he put a simple message in the personal column of four leading American newspapers. If Bolan did not contact him, Kurtzman then put similar ads in selected foreign newspapers and English-language papers around the world. Bolan had seen the ad in the *Los Angeles Times*. It said: "Mack come home. All is forgiven."

Bolan had called at 4:00 P.M. from the phone booth in front of the motel where he had been staying under simple disguise in California. He had dialed the number and listened as it rang three times. A connection was made to a dead-drop repeater, another three rings and another dead drop and then the call was forwarded. The phone had rung four times before someone picked it up.

"Yes?"

Neither phone was safe, neither one of them had the expensive and bulky scramblers they formerly used. Now it was catch as catch can. They had a simple code.

"Aaron, this is a friend."

"I hoped you would call."

Bolan had waited five beats. "How is everyone at the Farm?"

"Working. Always working."

If the ritual varied as much as a word, they both would hang up because someone would be with Kurtzman, or somehow the line had been tapped.

"It's clear here. Good to hear from you. I'm onto something I wanted you to know. Two years ago a top man at NASA quit in a huff. He wanted more emphasis on defensive, rather than offensive, missiles. Today I've seen a report that he has been pensioned off in Houston, given a new identity and also kept under twenty-four-hour observation, just as a safeguard."

"I remember something about him. A brilliant old guy, but a bit of a loner."

"That's him, Dr. Peter Dunning. Three weeks ago

our watchers found someone else watching him. They turned out to be a pair of low-echelon KGB agents. Everyone was trying to figure out what could be the connection between them. Yesterday Dr. Dunning left his house, ditched his Uncle Sam tail and the KGB, and vanished. Now the KGB duo is gone, too. Sounded like something you might be concerned about.''

"Might be."

"There's more. Last night somebody electronically captured an orbiting communications satellite and sent it crashing into the atmosphere over the East Coast just after dark. You probably heard about it."

"Yes." Bolan's mouth went dry. "If this guy could grab a satellite and dump it, why couldn't he do the same thing to any of our space hardware up there, including all of our spy-in-the-sky satellites?"

"Exactly, and with the KGB nosing around, I figured this might be one you'd want to know more about."

"I do. What else can you find out?"

"I can have a batch of printouts on Dunning in the morning. If you're interested you could catch the Red-Eye Express flight for Dulles and I'll meet you at the regular place tomorrow at 9:30 A.M. I'm working on a lead. Might have something for you on the site he used to make the snatch."

"Sounds interesting. I'll be there."

"See you tomorrow."

Bolan had said goodbye and grabbed his black aluminum suitcase. There was no Jack Grimaldi to fly him to Dulles, no Air Force jet to commandeer. He'd go tourist class to save money, and all of his dwindling supply of weapons would be in the suitcase.

He had packed a new Ingram M-10 he had picked up not long before, his .44 AutoMag and a Colt Commander .45 with extra loaded magazines for all three, and his last six fragmentation grenades. Luggage checked through was almost never searched. Not unless the owner gave some cause for alarm.

Bolan never did. He had fitted his black skinsuit and a few clothes into the bag, checked out of the motel and drove his rented car to Los Angeles from Laguna Beach where he had been staying.

He had decided to postpone his mission of finding a KGB mole working at the San Onofre Nuclear Power Generating Station. The word Bolan had was that the KGB planned on trying for three meltdowns at U.S. nuclear generating plants this year. But that would have to wait.

Bolan had made the Red-Eye with ten minutes to spare, checked his bag casually and slid into his aisle seat. He was asleep ten minutes after takeoff and woke only once before they landed at Dulles International Airport in Washington, D.C., the next morning.

Bolan had picked up his suitcase and had gone into the men's room. He shaved, applied a thick black mustache and a set of large, reflective sunglasses. He took out a brown wool cap that matched his sports coat and checked his suitcase in a locker. He had spent too much time in Washington, knew too many people there and knew many of them were searching for him. He needed some minimum disguise.

He had taken three taxis and half an hour later went to the Town and Country shopping center in Falls Church, Virginia. Once there, he had proceeded to the loading area behind the Safeway store. The blue van with the power tailgate sat parked away from the other cars as Kurtzman said it would. The license plate number was right. Bolan went to the driver's side and looked through the window. It rolled down, activated by a power switch. Bolan saw Kurtzman's grin.

"Get in—we'll go for a ride. I want to show you how well I can drive my new toy. They fixed it up for me with special hand brake, hand accelerator, the works. I've only had one fender bender since I got it."

On the seat beside Bolan lay a fat brown envelope. Kurtzman explained its contents to Bolan. It was filled with computer printouts and photographs.

"You're looking good, Mack. It's great to see you again."

"Same here, Aaron. You look as mean as ever." They shook hands and Kurtzman blinked rapidly and turned his head. Then he wiped a hand across his face and drove away.

"I got it confirmed this morning. NASA has a definite triangulation on the spot where the signals originated that knocked down the communications satellite. They're organizing a strike for first thing in the morning. Dawn. If you want to get there first, you'll have to leave here today. It's a small mesa about fifty miles southwest of Casa Grande, which is just below Phoenix, Arizona."

"Summarize all this, Aaron," Bolan said, holding up the packet.

"The man is brilliant, totally patriotic and dedicated. Quit because he didn't think he was doing enough for defense. No sign at all of any disloyalty. Speculation is that the KGB wants to grab him for his general knowledge of our missile systems and operations. Probably unrelated to current mischief.

"Problem: if he can capture a satellite and kill it, how much bigger U.S. hardware can he knock down?

"Problem: if the KGB does grab him, how much

damage could he do to the U.S. space program, thinking that he might be helping his dedication to antimissile defenses?"

"I hope you can find your way back to Dulles, Aaron. I'm going to have to hustle and see what kind of connections I can get into Phoenix." Bolan shook his head. "In the old days that would have been no problem—just call Jack Grimaldi and I'd be there in three hours."

"True, but here's something from the good old days. A test weapon. It's a Childers battle shotgun, a real banger. Don't even worry where it came from. I've still got friends at the Farm. It's wrapped up in a package back there, but it's only eighteen inches long. Take it with you for luck. Oh, there's also some double-ought buck rounds, couple of dozen. Now that's like the old days."

"I miss you guys, everybody," Bolan said.

"Dammit yes, we miss you, too. I used to complain that I had to walk so much between computers. Right now I'd give ten years' pay to walk that much."

"I know, Aaron."

"Like hell you do!" Kurtzman said with a flash of anger. "Nobody knows who hasn't been there." He looked over. "Sorry."

Mack punched Kurtzman's shoulder lightly. "Yeah, I'm sorry, too, and I swore that I'd waste every one of them who got away. I'm still working on it. I think I'll up the ante a little. Hey, are you sure you know the way to Dulles?"

Mack Bolan had flown out of Dulles at 1:00 P.M. on American, stopped in Salt Lake City for a connecting flight and arrived in Phoenix at 6:12. Plenty of time. He took out Kurtzman's penciled map, memorized it, then headed for the Hertz car rental counter.

3

Dr. Peter Dunning sat naked on the motel bed, totally relaxed. He had just taken a leisurely shower and was reveling in the air-conditioned coolness of his overnight accommodations. Even as he sat on the bed, he thought about his project. He had a secretary's spiral notebook in one hand and a pencil in the other as he made one last calculation.

Yes, it would work perfectly. There was no doubt in his mind now that he had the one last vital sensor. If Yamaguchi put in all of the groundwork they'd talked about, everything should be ready by tonight to start the serious instrument calibrations. Without those it would be hopeless.

He dropped the pad and dressed. Dr. Dunning hated the idea that scientists had to be long-haired and un-kempt. He was more of a fashion plate himself, always dressed well and made sure everything fit perfectly. That was vital.

Just as important as making sure that the program he fed into his computers would mesh precisely with the type of orders that some far-off orbiting black box had been programmed to receive.

No matter how clever he could be in his code-breaking, it would not mean a thing if the black box was not sent the exact instruction it needed to function. But he knew in detail everything that was needed, what he must produce to capture the orbiters.

Dr. Dunning finished dressing, packed his one small suitcase and checked the area critically. Nothing of value had been left behind, no identification of any kind. He had even wiped his fingerprints from the faucets, door handles and shower stall.

Now he was homing in on the last phase of that planning, his crowning achievement. He would go down in history. He would make sure of that in the next two days. Everything had to work properly. His dress rehearsal had played without a missed beat. He had no doubts that the actual performance would go as well.

The scientist smiled now, wondering how the Army, Air Force and NASA had made out storming his little hilltop "fortress." It had been an afterthought. He had flown in his electronic units by chopper to the small mesa and used two non-English speaking men for three days to set up the defenses. The men had not known what they were building, and he spoke to them through an interpreter, which suited him perfectly. The look on the faces of those troops storming the mesa would have been marvelous to see.

But now he did not have time to dwell on that. He had used the copter and flown his twin units off the mesa three days earlier, paid the pilot and loaded the gear on a truck trailer. Then he had deliberately hidden for a day, changed truck and trailer just in case the chopper pilot was contacted by police or NASA, and then he had driven on up to northern Arizona, where he was now, to his selected mission site.

Dr. Dunning checked the room once more, looked under the bed, in the bath and then in the closet. He had left nothing. Outside he put his suitcase into his Ford Bronco and slid into the driver's seat. The four-wheel-drive vehicle could go almost anywhere and had no trouble making it into his off-road location.

As he drove he reflected on how it all had happened. Ever since the first satellites had gone up, NASA, and probably the Russians as well, had devised methods to pirate the other's orbiters. At first there were rather simple methods to capture anything that was controlled by radio signals. The Russian satellites were out of contact with their Soviet controllers for two-thirds of their orbits.

During those periods in each orbit, the radio sensors on board would respond to anyone who sent the correct signal, the code. It was all a matter of unique wording and then regular changes. If an orbiter was captured, the one who stole it could change the access code so the former owner could not even "talk" with the machine in orbit.

In the beginning it was all one big international chess game, but then the stakes rose too high and NASA said no more capture games. We will leave your satellites alone if you keep your hands off ours. The unofficial truce had endured to the present day. But Dr. Dunning knew how to capture the Russian orbiters, and he was no longer bound by NASA agreements.

For months, then years, he had worried about the growing number of hydrogen offensive weapons available to each side. He was well aware that the silent, secret arms race was much more deadly and threatening than the public knew, or could even imagine.

The silent race was reaching fantastically deadly overkill proportions. And overkill was a word that defensive minds never used, did not even want to think about. They never utilized the principle in planning. More was better. Deadlier was better. Quicker was better. First strike was sacred. Overkill to the point of nonretaliation was nirvana.

Dr. Dunning wheeled the Bronco off the highway just outside Winslow and headed south on State 87 into the higher country where the trail would lead him through part of the Coconino National Forest and on into the Prescott National Forest. At Clints Well he turned north, taking a secondary road back toward Flagstaff. From there he would find his way on the slopes of Horse Knoll, a minor peak that stood almost seven thousand feet high.

Dr. Dunning drove fast and with confidence. He knew what his machine could do, he knew exactly where he was going. And he had made his decision to go on with his project. He had to stop the arms race. He would use his special talents to prove to the world just how horrendously dangerous these games were that the great powers were playing, and that they must cease now!

From time to time he had utilized the services of a solid, intelligent Japanese man. Sam Yamaguchi had been gardener, helper, man Friday, and even a kind of assistant for five years. Now he was driver, technician, assistant and gofer. For the past year Yamaguchi had been working full-time with Dr. Dunning on his current project.

The actual capture of the communications satellite had proved to be so simple that Dr. Dunning was disappointed. His biggest amusement had come in figuring exactly where to kick the satellite out of orbit so it would blaze like a comet across the eastern seaboard night sky. It had turned into a remarkable show.

A month earlier Dr. Dunning had picked out the perfect spot for the next phase of his project. He had found this bare knob on the side of Horse Knoll peak that would work beautifully. Enough trees remained at one side for cover, yet it contained an open area for the transmissions. For two days Yamaguchi and his two workers had been putting the trailer in the proper spot, raising the antenna and positioning it correctly and getting everything ready. Soon the wiring would be complete, and they would be set to begin the instrument calibration.

A short distance north of Clints Well, Dr. Dunning drove off the secondary highway onto a forestry road. For five miles he continued in four-wheel mode up the side of the mountain, through one locked gate, for which he had a key, and then on up a trail to a fallen tree that blocked his passage.

As if by magic two men ran out and pushed the top of the giant ponderosa pine to one side, opening a roadway through the tree. After he went through, Dr. Dunning saw the men replace the sections of the tree and vanish into the brush. Half a mile farther, through a heavily wooded section, he came to a stop near a big Kenworth highway diesel tractor. Just behind it was a thirty-foot utility trailer with fifth wheel. The trailer had been converted into Dr. Dunning's mobile launch/recovery/capture field headquarters.

The scientist swung down from the Bronco and greeted a slight, short Oriental who emerged from the trailer. His hair was cut in a World War II flattop style. He nodded, gave a hint of a bow, but when he spoke it was without smiling.

"Sir, our power supply has now reached a satisfactory level and the required cycle has stabilized. You can start testing instruments at your convenience."

"Thanks, Sam. I appreciate your good work." He

paused and something that had bothered him before surfaced. "Sam, you know I'm not a rich man, right? I've got a few dollars but nothing big. I told you I'd pay you as well as I could afford. Is that arrangement still agreeable?"

"Yes, sir. My men and I are well pleased."

Dr. Dunning heard the words, but somehow he tensed at the tone, at the way the words were said. Or was it just his imagination? His own nerves were acting up again. He nodded at Sam.

There was a lot of work he should be doing himself right now to get the instruments recalibrated, to get the electric output frozen at precisely the correct level and exactly on the right cycle. It was so critical that there be absolutely no margin for error. Yes, he must get started. Work now would put his final triumph that much closer.

He looked at Sam. Damn, he could not tell for sure just how the little Oriental man felt. He would never know. But so far it had worked out very well. Dr. Dunning turned from the Bronco and walked quickly toward the trailer. It was parked half under the pine trees and half out.

The side extending free of the pines had been painted with the usual black, green, brown and tan used in military camouflage. Some live treetops had been cut and positioned around, screening the rig further and making it virtually invisible from any side at more than a hundred yards.

On top of the closed end of the trailer sat the twelve-foot-diameter dish antenna. It had been transported inside the big trailer and had taken a full day to assemble and mount. After that, Dunning had checked it and tested it to be sure it was functioning properly for receiving. Now he would investigate the whole gamut of his telecommunications on the sending side.

Inside the trailer the control panels had been bolted to one wall and holes drilled into the roof for the antenna cables. At the near end were a sofa bed, two chairs and a small kitchen.

Dr. Dunning turned to the main console and seated himself in the swivel chair. He flipped on the power switch and checked the input level, then began pushing buttons, taking readings and noting the various combinations on the panels of functions that would all have to work in perfect concert for his project to succeed.

Basically it would be much like the grab of the communications ball, only tougher, because he had to work with the access codes that were a thousand times more complicated. He could never do it without the computer. With the computer-code possibility mode, the black box would zap the orbiter with forty thousand trigger codes on each try. He had captured the communications satellite with his five-thousand-possible-code transmission.

Sam Yamaguchi poked his head through the doorway, saw Dr. Dunning and went inside.

"It's all working well so far, Sam. The only problem I've found up to now is a minor voltage irregularity that we can fix in five minutes. Are you sure we have plenty of diesel fuel for the generator engine?"

"Yes, sir. We can run it continuously for five days."

"Fine. We just may need that many days if we don't hit our code quickly. I'm hoping that we get lucky."

"Should I put someone on an outpost for security?"

At times Sam lapped into military jargon, and Dr. Dunning had often thought of asking about his background, but never had. The whole military intellect had always puzzled and disturbed the missile man and probably always would. It was foreign and unnatural to Dr. Dunning.

"Yes, Sam. We agreed to have one man down by the fallen tree, especially if the forestry people come this way. We will need an early warning. We won't give them any reason to come up here, but they might. Then we'll be extremely quiet until they go away."

Yamaguchi nodded, turned and walked out of the trailer.

Dr. Dunning's face was animated as he went back to his work, getting everything aligned, calibrated and set for the job that was coming. With any luck at all they might get into some test-tracking action tonight as a warmup.

For a moment Dr. Peter Dunning laced his hands behind his head and stared at the trailer roof. He had begun this fight, and he would carry it through. For ten years he had been advocating a defensive system of anti-missile strength. He had been showing and proving his theories and arguing for a strong defense, rather than spending billions of dollars for a ridiculous overkill capability with nuclear warheads. But no one would listen to him.

Officially he had lost the fight, but he continued to propose, design and create for defensive purposes only. At last he had become counterproductive to the department. Everyone knew it and he did, too. He resigned. He had enough cash to live on for a few years. He pursued his hobby of peaceful uses of missiles and the defensive posture of U.S. missiles.

And now it had come to this. He would prove to the doubters; he would expose what was already up there; he would shame and pressure the big powers into telling the truth. He would blackmail them into it if he had to. He would win few points for his argument, but he would make the world a safer place in which to live. Of that he was totally convinced.

His own tactics? The communications satellite. A drop in the proverbial bucket. The firms that put it up could well afford the loss. It would all come out of taxes owed, or be covered by insurance. Either way there was no great actual loss. And what was more important, he had made a dramatic statement, a powerful demonstration of his power, and there had been no loss of human life.

Yes, life. That was what he held most sacred. And now he remembered that was one point he had been in conflict about with Sam, who had insisted he bring along his personal weapon, an old Army issue .45-caliber automatic that he had owned for many years. Sam kept talking about the danger of bears in this wilderness.

Bears? They had not seen any, but Dr. Dunning was sure that Sam had brought his gun. The scientist did not like pistols. He had never fired one and would never have one in his house or on his project. Guns kill things—animals and people.

He sighed. One more run-through on the board and a final set of calibration tests and he would be ready to wait until late tonight for a test. Then he could start his experimental tracking. The measurements had to be precise. He would see to that.

Dr. Dunning smiled as he worked over his console, almost caressing the buttons, monitoring the dials and the readouts. Just a few more hours and the whole world would know what he was trying to do—what he *would do*!

4

Mack Bolan had driven hard north into Phoenix. He met a convoy of twenty Army vehicles coming toward him when he was ten miles away from the mesa. They did not stop. In Phoenix he found State 17 and powered on north, heading for Flagstaff and then east on Highway 40 to Winslow, a small town of nine or ten thousand people, where he hoped to pick up the strings of his search of Dr. Peter Dunning.

It was Arizona hot. The car radio reported that it was 104 degrees in Phoenix. The Executioner had examined the slip of paper that he had found in the generator and radio shack on the mesa. The rubber stamp impression had been some kind of an inspector's approval, but the ball-point-pen numbers and words caught his imagination, even though they did not mean anything to him at once.

The words were "cyclic," "base," "monitor" and "elliptical." He could put all sorts of meanings and combinations of meanings to the words, but none of them provided any clues. He still needed to know where Dr. Dunning had moved. Winslow might prove to be a dud, but it was the only possibility he had left. The numbers on the paper were as baffling as Dunning's disappearance.

They were: "14.16 PQ x 2," "115 to 120," "22,000" and "the square root of 22,000 (or 148.32396)." The first set meant nothing to him. The 115 to 120 could be voltage—common, regular household and business voltage that Dr. Dunning could be using on his computer and radio gear. Twenty-two thousand was used twice, and the only thing he could think of was a note in the paper that had indicated the communications satellite had been in a parking orbit at twenty-two thousand miles over the earth. Which left him nowhere. Since the orbiting altitude meant nothing to Bolan, the square root of that number meant even less.

He relaxed behind the wheel, pumped the rented Ford up to sixty-five and cruised on to Winslow. The town was high, dry and hot. It was on the tourist-trade route, and there were lots of air-conditioned motels to choose from. The thought was especially inviting since Bolan had already been up for the past twenty-eight hours. He wheeled down the one-way main street until he found the Stag and Stallion.

He parked a couple of blocks past the tavern, walked back and entered the building.

Inside it was the usual beer bar, air conditioned, with stand-up rail, stools and booths. The TV screen was tuned to the sports channel, and Bolan had noticed an eight-foot-diameter satellite dish antenna on the roof of the establishment. It was free satellite-broadcast TV until they started scrambling the signal.

There were six men at the bar, eyes glued to the big screen, watching a Mexican lightweight take apart a young black puncher.

Bolan straddled a stool and signaled for a mug of draft beer. He looked around. It was plainly a working-man's hangout, with a garish oil painting of a reclining nude over the mirror behind the bar.

The bartender, with a spotty apron around his middle, brought the draft beer. Bolan paid for the drink and worked on it slowly as he listened to the conversation at the bar. There was nothing about satellites. Nothing about a truck or a mad scientist. There would not be.

The barman came back to Bolan. "Another one, sport?"

"Yeah, soon as I take care of this one. Hey, I'm looking for my buddy, Red Andrews. Drives a semi with a forty-foot reefer. Supposed to be waiting for me here on one of your stools."

Before the barkeep had time to answer, Bolan caught one of the customers staring at him in the mirror. The man looked away quickly when Bolan's gaze locked with his.

"He ain't here. We get lots of semis through. Drivers don't come in here much. Your best bet is to check Parson's Pit Stop station west of town. Got room for the big semis out there. They pump diesel and they got a damn greasy spoon. Best truck stop we got."

"Thanks," Bolan finished the beer.

"You come back with Red for a few beers tonight, hear? We got a local topless dancer comes in at ten and shakes them around a little. She ain't bad."

"Just might be back."

Bolan slid off the stool and went outside. The hot air hit him like an angry blowtorch. He walked the couple of blocks to his car and slid behind the wheel. As he shut his door he checked his rearview. A man came out of the bar and looked around. It was the same guy in a tan work shirt who had watched Bolan in the mirror. A hunch, that was all. But Bolan had lived this long partly by playing his hunches.

He watched the man study the street, then Bolan started the car and eased out into the sparse daytime traffic. He turned west into a street that headed out of town. Bolan kept glancing at his rearview closely and saw the tan-shirt man jump into an ancient pickup and spin rubber following him.

Bolan nodded. If you can't find them, let them find you. Except in this case he had no idea who was on his tail. Bolan drove slowly enough for the red truck to get closer.

Then he speeded up, whipped through the railroad underpass on a street that soon wound into the sparsely populated high country. The Executioner had to know how serious this man was, and what he was after. A few words of polite conversation over the muzzle of the Ingram should do the trick.

Bolan kept the needle around forty and saw the pickup boiling up at him at half again that speed. The "old" pickup was a disguise. It must have a powerful V-8 under the sheet metal.

Bolan thrust his foot down on the accelerator. The rented Ford fishtailed a moment, then went charging down the narrow blacktop. There were no houses or ranches here. The country was high and dry with small mesas, rocks and sand with little vegetation, not even sagebrush.

He turned onto the next dirt lane to the left and pushed the gas pedal down, sending a thick dust pall spewing up behind him to slow down the pursuing vehicle.

Bolan fished the Ingram from a well-worn black case beside him and made sure its magazine was in place. He charged the weapon so it was ready to fire. Then he slowed, tugged on the wheel and hit the brakes at just the right second to put the Ford into a 180-degree sliding turn. He stopped, the vehicle pointing back the way he had come, facing a blinding dust storm from his own tires.

He did not have to wait long.

The red pickup came creeping through the dust, stopped abruptly and the engine died. Bolan had left his car by the passenger door and now peered over the roof. He could not see the driver.

"What the hell are you doing bird-dogging me?" Bolan snarled.

His answer was a booming shot from a handgun. The slug pinged off Bolan's car, missing him by a hair-breadth. He could feel himself going into an icy rage. Okay, sucker, let's do it. He ducked and looked under his Ford. He could see his attacker's feet and legs under the high frame of the pickup. Bolan sent a blistering round from the Ingram under the two rigs at the gun-man's ankles.

When the chatter of the shots died away, Bolan heard an anguished bellow of pain and fury. He saw a man slumped in the dirt at the far side of the truck.

"Throw your piece into the road," Bolan growled.

There was a scream of anger, frustration. Then a hand-gun sailed over the pickup and landed in the roadway.

"Good, now lie down in the dirt, hands laced on top of your head." Bolan watched under his car until he saw the man had complied, then the Executioner ran to the side of the truck and went cautiously around the tailgate.

The man was lying on his back in the powder-fine Arizona dirt, his face contorted with pain, tears rolling down his cheeks. Bolan figured he was about thirty-five. Bolan moved forward slowly and held the Ingram ready as he frisked the man. He found no more weapons. One of the gunman's ankles was bleeding. His foot stuck out at a strange angle to his leg.

"Why the hell were you following me?"

The bushwhacker stared up, grasping his leg above the bloody part as he groaned in pain. Sweat beaded his forehead. His defiant green eyes wavered. His hair was cut short, and he wore the black uniform pants of a factory man. He was slender and about six feet tall.

"Hell, that hurts! You shot me! Busted my ankle. I'm gonna bleed to death."

"Why did you shoot at me?"

"Why? Somebody paid me to listen for anybody asking questions, any strangers asking about trucks."

"Like me."

"Uh-huh. Now get me to a goddamned doctor! My ankle is all shot to hell, and I'm bleeding like a stuck shoat."

Bolan looked at the bleeding ankle. There was too much blood. He used his handkerchief and made a pad, which he pressed against the major wound. The man howled in pain.

"Better than bleeding to death. Take off your shirt." Bolan tore two strips from the shirt and bound the ankle wound until the blood stopped flowing. He sat back and scowled at the man.

"You're lucky to be alive, asshole!" Bolan snapped. "You come up shooting again at a stranger, and you probably will catch one in your useless head. Who is this man you work for?"

"Can't tell you. Goddammit, I need a doctor for my ankle!"

"True, but if you don't tell me the man's name you'll have to walk, crawl or hitchhike back to town." Bolan turned and strode away.

"No!" the man screamed in panic. "Please don't go.

I'll tell you. His name is Sam Yamaguchi. He's a short Japanese guy with a flattop haircut."

"How old?"

"Thirty, thirty-five. He's new in town."

"Where can I find him?"

"You can't. I can't. He phones me every night about six at the bar back there. He won't tell me where he is. Once I heard the operator tell him to deposit eighty-five cents for the first three minutes. So it was long distance, but not too far away. Oh, that hurts. Take me into town!"

"Why did you shoot at me?"

"That 180-degree slide you did. That was too damn good. I figured you was a cop. I'm on parole and I had a piece. Automatic reaction, I guess. Let's go."

"You see the big truck?"

"Hell, no. It went through town three, four days ago. I met this Yamaguchi guy two days ago. He's somewhere around nearby. Maybe back in the hills if he's hiding something. Now get me to the damn doctor!"

"Okay. Get into your own rig. Passenger side."

Bolan half carried him to the door and helped him in. The man screamed only once getting his right foot in the door, then nearly passed out.

Bolan took the keys and eased the red pickup into the sharp ditch and spun the tires until it was stuck. He got out and looked in through the window. The guy was sweating but not because of the 104-degree July heat.

"I'll tell the cops I saw your truck ditched out here. They should be around in ten minutes. If that man calls you again, you never saw me, understand? You breathe one word about this and I'll return. Only next time I'll aim higher."

The man stared at the icy blue eyes of death that

bored into him, and he had no doubt that he was close to dying. He shivered and nodded.

"Yes, sir. I won't tell him nothing. No, sir. You can count on that." He was trembling. "Hell, that leg hurts!" He stared at the Ingram Bolan still carried.

Bolan walked away, got into his Ford and drove back to town. At the first phone booth he placed a call to the local police without giving his real name. Then he drove on, looking for Parson's Pit Stop.

It was crowded. The Executioner pulled up next to a pump and filled his tank. As he paid for it his eyes scanned the area, observing and evaluating everything in a casual survey. There were several big rigs there, but the one the Japanese man was protecting would not be one of them. The Oriental must be tied in with Dr. Dunning.

After gassing up, Bolan drove to the side of the big lot, backed into a parking space, and pretended to take a nap, pulling a baseball cap down over his eyes, but leaving a sight line out to watch the Pit Stop action.

He slid the Ingram in the case and pushed his Colt Commander in his belt clip-on holster under his sport shirt.

Bolan felt he was wasting his time. He did not have much to go on. An eighty-five-cent long-distance call. That would extend maybe twenty miles out of town. He got out of the car and walked to the diesel pumps. There were two of them, and six semis were lined up to take on fuel.

Bolan found the attendant and talked with him.

"Hell, yes, most of my customers are regulars. They got a three- or four-day run, so they come by here once, twice a week. Them guys is what keep us in business."

"What about strangers? Get many one-timer semis?"

"Sure, but usually it's like now—all six of these guys are regulars."

"Looking for a buddy of mine, little Japanese guy with a flattop haircut. Should have been through here three or four days ago."

"Damn. There are so many guys in and out. What's a flattop?"

"Short haircut, like a crew cut but the top of it is ruler flat. Lots of them back in World War II. Named the haircut after the big aircraft carriers."

"Oh, them. Yeah, I seen this guy you're talking about. He was in here last week. I remember because he was so damn touchy about his trailer. Wouldn't let me near it."

"Was it a Mack diesel?"

"Hell, no, brand-new Kenworth, big one with lots of chrome and a sleeper. I told him he had too much tractor for that thirty-footer he was dragging. He just ignored me. Uppity mother."

"That sounds like my buddy, Sam. Did he keep on going down Interstate 40 out here?"

"Nope. The little bastard got all friendly the next minute and asked me about the roads into the hills to the south. He wanted State 87, so I told him how to get on it. Strange character. Something about his eyes I didn't like. Scary, you know?"

"I've seen them. Thanks. You're a big help. Oh, has anyone else been asking about my buddy, Sam? Some credit guy is after him."

"There was somebody in here this morning looking for a semi, but they didn't know if he was Japanese, or anything about his rig. I told them lots of luck. Your friend must owe a bundle on that semi."

"He does. Thanks." Bolan walked back to his car.

So, someone else was on Dunning's trail. It couldn't be Uncle Sam. Those government people were still playing around with the mesa below Phoenix.

The Executioner at least had some kind of direction. The rig was headed down Highway 87. Now all he had to know was the radius you could call for eighty-five cents.

Bolan unlocked his car and slid inside. He started the engine and drove onto the highway. He'd find the phone company or just a booth and give the operator his question. She would know the toll zones by heart.

About half a mile along, he spotted a coffee shop on the highway and pulled in beside two telephone booths. He turned off the engine and was reaching for the door when he felt the cold steel of a gun muzzle pressed against his neck.

5

"Please do not do anything rash," a woman's voice said from the back seat. "This is loaded and goes off quite easily. I really do not want you dead, so just relax and keep your hands on the steering wheel where I can see them."

Mack Bolan never argued with a gun pressed against his neck. He sat quietly in the front seat of his car and put both hands slowly on the steering wheel. When he tried to find the woman's image in the rearview mirror, he could not.

"This is a poor place to rob somebody, lady."

"I am not going to rob you. Just relax, do not attempt anything foolish and you will remain alive."

Bolan heard a car pull in beside them. The door slammed, and a man opened Bolan's front passenger door and slid in. He picked up Bolan's weapons case and passed it to the woman in the back seat. Bolan digested the newcomer's features and ran them through his mental computer files. But he couldn't get a make on the man. He was in his forties with black hair, a stiff squared-off jaw, dark brown eyes and a mean expression. He wore sports clothes draped over a squat torso with a bulge of a weapon under the tail of his Hawaiian print shirt.

"No trouble so far," the woman said. "Your turn."

With a hamlike hand the man drew a short-barreled revolver from his belt and pressed it into Bolan's side.

"Hey, easy!" Bolan yelped, trying to give a good impression of fright. "Keep that thing away from me! It could hurt somebody. What the hell you people doing, anyway? I was just trying for a little nap after I gassed up, and then I talked with the pump man for some facts about his operation here. I want to do a free-lance article about truck stops. The Pit Stop is a good one."

"Shut up!" the man said in heavily accented English. "Be quiet. We know what you talked to the attendant about: Dr. Dunning. We, too, are interested in the good scientist and want to find him as much as you do."

"What scientist? I'm doing an article for *Commercial Car Journal*."

The man's hand darted to Bolan's belt and snaked out the .45 Colt Commander from the holster.

"Then why do you carry this big gun? Let us get down to the truth. We know you look for Dr. Dunning. We want to learn what you have found out, and we will get the information from you one way or another. First we drive into the desert where we can have more privacy."

Without looking at the woman, he got out and closed his door, went around the car and pushed Bolan into the passenger's side. Then the hijacker drove the car down Highway 40 for five miles, finally pulling off onto a desert track that led across the barren landscape. Bolan could see the gentle rise of the hills to the south.

The woman held her gun on Bolan's neck as they drove. When they stopped the man pushed him out the side door, slammed him against the side of the car and frisked him. They found the knife in Bolan's boot, but missed the small blade behind his belt.

Then the man spun Bolan around and slashed the Colt Commander down across the side of his head. The

Executioner saw it coming and pivoted away from the blow, but caught enough of it to rip a gash on his forehead. The force of the impact was enough to drop Bolan to his knees in the sand.

They had driven a half mile off the main road and stopped behind a small hill. They were in a totally secluded area.

"Strip," the man ordered. "Take off all your clothes and your shoes. Do it right now."

For the first time Bolan saw the woman. She was slender, tall, with short, soft blond hair and a pretty face. He figured she was about thirty. She held a 9mm Luger as if she knew how to use it. The stern expression on her face told him she would not hesitate to fire the weapon.

"Hey, take it easy. I don't know anything about a guy named Dunning. I'm doing the damn truck-stop story!"

The man tried to kick Bolan in the crotch but the Executioner jumped away, taking the blow on the side of his thigh. He was ready to counter the thrust when he realized either one of them could shoot him if he attacked now.

Slowly he nodded. "You've got the guns. So I strip, what then?"

"Then we see if you are a CIA agent," the woman said. "Most agents have many scars on their bodies. We think you will have them, too."

"Sure I have scars. I was shot a few times in Vietnam. But I'm not a CIA agent. I never have been. I worked for the government when I was drafted, but that's all over now, thanks to the KGB." Bolan watched closely and the man's right eye twitched. It was enough. "I'm strictly a civilian. I don't work for any government agency. Which is more than the two of you can say.

KGB, lower ranks. As a journalist I can smell you people a mile away. Has the Kremlin run out of good talented spies? Laughing boy here would be the more experienced, and our sweet little blonde is the mole, recently dug up for this mission. Hell, must be damn important.''

"Strip," the man snarled.

Bolan took off his clothes quickly, naturally, until he was naked. He turned toward the woman. "I don't imagine that you're going to strip down, too?"

The blow came slightly before Bolan expected it, a massive fist into the back of his neck, driving him to his knees.

"How much do you know about Dr. Dunning?" the woman asked.

"His name—that's all you've told me so far."

The man's toe stung Bolan's side, aiming for his kidney. It missed.

"Save yourself a lot of punishment, American. We know you talked to the filling-station man about the truck and the Japanese driver. We could overhear that much. So now cooperate with us and do not lie. There is no reason for us to spill any of your blood."

Bolan glanced up and she was in front of him, looking him up and down. She smiled.

"American, tell us what you know about Dr. Dunning," she said again, her tone more pleasant.

Bolan had been doing a quick recalculation. They knew he was on the problem. He would tell them what they already must have learned to be this far along the trail. And perhaps save himself some unnecessary punishment.

"I don't know any more than you do. He's brilliant, he worked for NASA until two years ago, and now he's off on his own. He captured and knocked down a U.S. communications satellite that cost something like twenty million dollars. Now I think he's in this area somewhere. How did you get this far along on his tracks?''

"We ask the questions," the man said, kicking Bolan in the back. The Executioner groaned for effect.

"What else did the filling-station attendant tell you?''

"That diesel gives better mileage than gasoline," Bolan said. He anticipated the kick from the left side this time. He spun on his knees, caught the boot, rammed it upward with his left hand and smashed his right fist with all his power into the Russian's crotch.

The man screamed in pain as he pawed for his pistol. Bolan surged upright as the agent bellowed his rage again and fell, the agony of his crushed testicles sapping his strength, dropping him to the ground. He pulled up his knees to his chest to try to relieve the grinding, excruciating pain in his scrotum.

A shot slammed through the dry air and missed Bolan by inches. He dived behind the writhing hulk of the Russian, grabbed him by the throat and peered around him at the woman.

She held the Luger, a frown on her pretty face as she looked for a target.

"Drop it, lady, or I tear out his carotid arteries and he dies in twenty seconds.''

"Unlikely. A difficult kill. Even if you can do it, I would wait until Niki is dead, then I shoot you as you leave his body.''

"You can try. But by then I'll have my .45 back, and I'll be blasting you straight into hell.'' Bolan tightened his grip around the man's throat, shutting off the air until he began coughing and gagging. When Bolan looked at the Russian woman again, she was impassive.

"You are wrong, American. I was not the mole— neither of us was. We are both on this special assignment. We have known for nearly a month that your Dr. Dunning was going to try to sabotage our missiles. We thought he was doing it with your government's backing. Now we find he is entirely on his own." She lifted her beautifully arched brows. "Perhaps you are working for Dunning." She paused, then shook her head. "No, no. Then you would know where to find him." She sighed and brought up her pistol. "Be realistic, American. If you kill Niki, I shall have to kill you. An eye for an eye, a corpse for a corpse."

"Why?" Bolan asked. "Just because he was stupid enough to make a mistake and give me an opening to attack? He isn't in your class, lady, that's clear. You are the senior agent, right? He was your muscle and not very smart muscle at that." Bolan let off the pressure around the Russian's throat so he could breathe normally.

"You said you knew a month ago that Dunning was going to do this?"

"Yes, and we began to track him. But your Dr. Dunning is a clever man."

"He's also a pacifist, as you must know. He wants to outlaw war and violence, do away with all offensive weapons. That's why he quit our space agency. And it could be that he's planning to attack both our nations' space missiles. Do something to draw attention to the problem, get worldwide attention. The way he dramatically knocked down that communications satellite might be what he is planning on a grander scale."

"He is a dangerous man."

"Or one too brilliant for his time."

"I am beginning to get an idea, American," she said.

"I hope it's the same one I'm getting."

"If you promise not to kill Niki, we can talk about working together for the common good, to stop this madman from damaging our orbiting satellites."

Bolan nodded. "If we have anything to pool, we will. I know little besides what I told you."

She smiled and lowered the Luger. "You know more, much more. That was obvious the crude way you lied to Niki—a normal ploy." She looked at him closely, then lowered the pistol to her side.

"I agree to cooperate if you do. I have little to lose. Niki and I were at a dead end here. We could go no further. I know that Dr. Dunning and three men went through here three days ago. He had a diesel tractor, a thirty-foot trailer and a four-wheel-drive utility vehicle. We are not sure where he went from here. We believe his entire scientific equipment for his space theft is contained in the two vehicles."

She gathered up Bolan's clothes and carried them to him.

"Partners?" she asked. "We do not have to like or trust each other, just work together on this mission. All agreements are off once we have stopped this madman."

Bolan eased his hands away from the Russian's throat as he watched the woman.

The Executioner hesitated for a second before he spoke.

"Your people killed my woman, cut her down without a chance. She wasn't even in a combat situation. She put herself in the line of fire to help...."

"My father was KGB, one of the first. One of the best. An American agent strangled him in West Germany with his bare hands. I, too, have some anger."

She bent and laid his clothes beside him. Bolan let go of Niki.

"If we work together, can you control this Cro-Magnon maniac?"

"Niki will do as I tell him."

"No!" The roaring denial came as the man rolled away from them both, drawing the automatic from his belt. Bolan was up and dodging, darting toward the Russian. The .45 roared into the desert air, but the round missed. Niki rolled again and Bolan was almost on top of him but the lightweight Colt Commander swung up again in the Russian's hand. There was nowhere to dodge, no time, no place, no chance.

For a frozen second in time Bolan stared into the round black hole of his own .45. He was looking death in the face and he knew it. He heard a shot even as he lunged to the side. He hit the hot sand and rocks on his bare shoulder, then rolled, realizing that he wasn't dead. He jumped up, still naked, and stared down at the writhing form of Niki in the red dust. A fountain of blood spurted from his neck.

In a montage of sight, sound and time moving in slow motion, Bolan saw the Luger tracking up again. This time the hot lead ripped through Niki's forehead, blasting him backward into the rocks and soil, canceling another Soviet agent from their roster.

Bolan stared at the female Russian agent.

She shrugged. "He disobeyed me. It was the least he could expect. I have not been happy with him as a partner during the past month. We should have caught Dunning by now." She waved her hand and put the pistol away. "This one was of no importance. Put your clothes on and we will talk. Perhaps we each have something the other could use." She studied him frankly, the double meaning coming through plainly to Bolan.

He dressed. She picked up the Colt and handed it to Bolan. Then she removed the fake identification from Niki's pockets and they walked to the car.

"There is no use to hide the body. We will be gone by the time anyone finds him. I shall report his demise to my superiors. They expect some losses."

They sat in his rented Ford and Bolan looked at her.

"You saved my life back there. He had me cold. There was no way I could have stayed alive. I don't even know your name."

"In English it is like the name Kitty."

He looked at her more carefully, saw a firm jaw, soft blue eyes and short blond hair that seemed exactly right for her. She was pretty, a year or two older than the thirty he had first guessed. She smiled. "Kitty, why did you shoot Niki? You had to make up your mind quickly."

"He was about to kill my best lead to Dr. Dunning. He was acting out of personal anger and pain. He was out of his head—how do you say—crazy, and he had to be liquidated. And I know you found out something more from the filling-station man. With what you have and what we have, we can find Dr. Dunning. I shot Niki because he was wrong, and because he went against my leadership once too often."

Bolan decided he could work with this woman until the mission was over, but no more. She had saved his skin, and he owed her that much.

He suppressed his constant boiling fury at the KGB and its operation that claimed April Rose. Somehow he had to keep under control his deep-seated killing vengeance. Later he would fight the other battle.

The Executioner drove back to town, found another filling station that had telephones and went to the first one. He asked the operator the question and she had a quick answer.

"An eighty-five-cent call from here could go to only three or four areas: Flagstaff, Holbrook or Clints Well to the south, and of course into the reservations. There may be a few more spots, but most of them would be ranches and private homes. That's the radius for an eighty-five-cent toll call."

Bolan held the phone so Kitty could hear. She frowned as they got back into the car. He explained to her about the man with the gun and the red pickup and Sam Yamaguchi.

"The call was always long distance, and once he heard the operator ask for him to put in the eighty-five cents. We have a range of about thirty to forty miles three ways. We won't go back to Flag, and Holbrook doesn't seem right, if you want to hide all that equipment. Dunning seems to like the wide-open spaces. I'd pick Clints Well as our next stop. Besides, the station attendant said Yamaguchi asked how to get to Highway 87. That goes south into the mountains and to Clints Well."

"Yes, I knew you had more than I did." She watched him with a soft smile. They were sitting close together in the car and the contact was not unpleasant for Bolan.

"First, what shall I call you?" she said. "What name?"

"Mack, call me Mack. It's a good cover name."

"Very well. Mack, you make decisions quickly yourself. I like that. Are you certain this is the best direction to take?"

"Highway 87 goes north directly into the Apache and

Hopi Indian reservations. A lot of dry mesas and no cover. He's south. Let's check the map in the car. I've seen most of this country before. If I had the choice, I'd go to the mountains. The more height he has, the better his contact with the stars. The more mountains, the harder to find him and the easier to defend. Besides, the gas-station man said he asked how to get south.''

Kitty lifted her brows and slowly nodded. ''Yes, it sounds reasonable, practical. I will go along with your suggestion.''

They drove back to her parked rental car, took her two suitcases from the trunk and transferred them to Bolan's wheels. Two minutes later they were driving out of Winslow, heading south on 87 into the mountains.

6

As he drove, Bolan occasionally glanced at the enemy agent. He could not stop wondering if he had made the right decision. So far she had brought nothing to the co-operative effort. Stark, terrible memories flooded through him of Stony Man Farm on that fateful day when all hell had broken loose.

The KGB had tried to kill the man they knew as Colonel John Phoenix. They missed him, but in the terrible fight they had brutally, needlessly, snuffed out the life of April Rose.

Bolan felt his anger surge. He sucked in a quick breath, and his hands tightened around the steering wheel. He had made a vow that day to avenge April's death. Whoever was responsible would die for that attack, and for those loved ones disabled and gone forever.

Again, the Executioner was a fugitive, operating outside the law, hunted from every side, but still he fought the battle against Animal Man and his crimes against humanity. Bolan did not care whether the adversary was the Mafia, terrorists, or some other greater evil that jeopardized the freedom of the common man. The Executioner's future would be written in blood—the enemy's blood.

The feeling of being one man alone against the world came through strongly to him again. It was more intense than ever; it kept him sharper and more on his toes. It made his combat skills vital to his existence. At times he felt like a mouse in a meadow filled with hungry wild-cats, hawks and coyotes.

It all made him more determined than ever to con-tinue the fight until he had either won each individual battle or perished in his best attempt.

However, there was zero margin for error.

She saw him glance at her and smiled.

"Still wondering if you made the right decision to team up with me? I am sure you did, Mack. We can work well together, and when this is over, we will decide what comes next. Until then we must be a team, operate as a military unit. We must defend each other, protect each other, think alike. True, I saved your life an hour ago, but next it may be your turn to save mine. We do not know yet just what we face up here."

Bolan nodded, realizing what she said on the surface and for the mission was true. Trust and support as on any team. But he must never forget whom she worked for.

Bolan breathed deeply and tried to relax his hands on the wheel. He sat back in the driver's seat and put his left hand at the bottom center of the wheel. It was less tension-producing that way.

He blinked and shook his head. There was no time for sleep now. He could go for at least forty-eight hours without sleep, but only if he concentrated. The mind could force the body to obey, but only if that mind was strong enough. Bolan's was. He concentrated and the sleep need faded, and he was in total command again.

It had not always been that way. He had joined the army early in the Vietnam conflict, not content to wait to be drafted, eager to get the battle won and the boys home again. In the Army he had excelled in basic training and soon joined the Special Forces and trained to be a paratrooper, sniper and underwater expert. He had ranked first or second in every school he attended.

In Vietnam he had refined his natural combat sense and quickly became a specialist in missions behind enemy lines. During his tours of duty in Nam he had won the Bronze Star, two Purple Hearts and a Silver Star.

He developed into an expert assassin who could penetrate Cong defenses and camps to waste high military officials. He was a deathbringer. His true nature as a natural combatman surfaced at once in Nam. He had been labeled with the title of "Executioner" in that far-off land when he completed his long string of successful kills of Vietcong and North Vietnamese officers. They lost track after ninety-seven such missions.

But he was also known among the civilians of Vietnam as "Sergeant Mercy," because of his genuine and deep-seated concern for the country's civilians. He understood that they were the real victims of that total war. He went out of his way to safeguard the locals and often did it at a high risk to his own life.

While in Vietnam he exposed and wiped out a black-market and extortion ring that three American GIs were running in Tran Ninh province.

Then his father died by his own hand, and Bolan flew home on an emergency leave only to find that his father had not only killed himself, but Bolan's sister, Cindy, and their mother. Only Bolan's younger brother, Johnny, survived. The root cause of it all was the Mob. That began the Executioner's long war against the Mafia, which lasted for thirty-eight blood-drenched campaigns.

Then the thrust of his efforts changed. Not really by

choice. Some said he had had a choice. However, five federal agencies wanted his scalp on a platter and police in twenty-one states and hundreds of local jurisdictions had arrest warrants for him.

The Man said Bolan had a choice. He could continue his war against the Mafia and know his odds of capture were running thin, or he could come in out of the cold and work for the U.S. government. Quickly he had a presidential pardon, which was and would remain top secret.

The federal people had orchestrated a violence-filled, fiery death for Mack Bolan in New York City's Central Park. Plastic surgery followed, giving him a different look, and he was provided with a completely new identity and background.

The Phoenix program was started with Stony Man Farm as its command center. He was Colonel John Phoenix, U.S. Army, retired. Hell, for a while there Bolan had felt great not being a wanted man anymore, having some clout and respect as a full-bird colonel and not always being on the run.

Then the undeniable will and power of the KGB had won a round with the attack on the Farm and the death of April Rose. The Soviet terror machine had created a Colonel John Phoenix double and staged a political assassination in public of an important European labor leader.

Then John Phoenix was definitely identified as the killer. Even the U.S. authorities suspected Bolan had made the hit. It was done that well. At once Bolan was cut off from government sanction and was actively sought as a rebel, a turncoat, an outlaw who had turned against his country and doublecrossed the generosity, the wisdom and the orders of Uncle Sam.

Once more, Mack Bolan was a fugitive.

Mack Bolan was free to do battle with any enemy he chose. He did not take assignments from the government to fight terrorists. He could aim his wrath and vengeance at anyone, anywhere, at any time. And high on his hit list was the KGB and its thousands of operatives. Those terrormongers who had cut down April Rose would always be his number-one enemy.

And he had targets. While in Russia he had obtained a list of KGB agents, their operations and activities in every country in the world. But now he was sitting beside a KGB agent, cooperating with one. For a while.

But for all the changes, the battle the Executioner fought was still the same: a life-and-death struggle against fear and frustration brought on by the continuing, unrelenting fight against the enemy—Animal Man in all his manifestations.

Bolan had to endure, and at the same time as a thinking individual he had to justify his motives and his actions. But over and through it all came the ultimate factor: in order to fight and win against evil, he had first to survive. That was the ultimate factor—survival. Without that, there was simply the ending, the blackness of death, the long sleep with no dreams.

Bolan shook his head, breathed deeply again and checked the summertime midafternoon highway ahead of him. Empty. Little traffic. They were now climbing gradually into the hills. They would climb two thousand feet as they went. It was cooler already as they came into the first of the tall pines.

The Executioner glanced at his companion. Kitty had put her head against the seat back and slept. Her face in repose was vulnerable. Gone was the sternness, the hard quality that he had found so characteristic of people in her line of work. Her brows twitched with REM and Bolan wondered what she was dreaming about.

One hour later, Bolan pulled the car into an isolated roadside café. It would get little traffic, and the owners would be on duty as long as it was open. They might have heard something, seen something. Besides, he was hungry. As soon as the car slowed, Kitty awoke with no grogginess. Her hand fell to her purse and she glanced at him.

"Trouble?"

Bolan shook his head. "Only hunger pangs. Lunch?"

"Yes, and we can make some subtle probings about...." She paused and laughed softly. "I am sorry. You obviously thought of that while I was sleeping. I will not try to direct our operation." She frowned slightly. "But on important matters, I expect consultation, input and approval before we move."

Bolan stopped the car at the wooden-rail fence in front of the café and nodded. "I'll always do that, especially when you're dead to the world."

"Mack, you may be a difficult person to work with."

"True, but then I tend to reflect the personalities of those I'm teamed with. Consultation: shall we have something to eat?"

She nodded, smiling. "I concur, but only if it is a hamburger or something truly American."

The little eatery had six stools along the counter and three booths crowded in the corner. Bolan and Kitty chose a booth. Hamburgers were on the top of the menu, painted on a board over the window into the kitchen. A woman in her thirties grabbed a couple of glasses, filled them with ice water and came over, a big smile on her ruddy face.

"Hello, folks. Shore glad you stopped by. Y'all want coffee now while you pick out your supper?"

"Yes, that would be fine," Bolan said. Kitty looked at him in surprise. When the waitress left, Kitty whispered to Bolan.

"That is a Deep South accent. What is she doing this far to the West."

"It's a free country, remember? Our people are not tied down to one section or region or job. You must have learned that."

"Yes, of course. Still, it does seem strange."

They both had New York-cut steak dinners, deciding they might not be able to eat again for a long time. As they waited for their meal, Bolan talked to the waitress-cook who was also half owner of the café.

"Yep, we get a few semis through here now and then. This ain't what you'd call the main road to Phoenix, know what I mean? And you say you're on this special treasure hunt trying to follow a big semi Kenworth tractor. Hey, I know Kenworth. My ex-man drives one. His has a sleeper. That's why he's my ex. He kept picking up them high-school runaway girls and shared his sleeper with them. But I shore don't remember no Kenworth and a small Japanese man driving through here. Lordy, I ain't seen me a flattop haircut in ten years, more or less."

When the steaks came they were tender and rare, with red juices running out with each knife cut. Bolan watched Kitty eating. She looked up at him.

"Yes, all right, I love steak. We do not get much at home. I must admit that your common people eat much better than ours. We just think other things are more important."

"Bombs, not butter," Bolan said. She shrugged and went back to the steak. She finished the meal well before he did, eating every scrap on her plate. Bolan paid the check, and they walked back to the car. A road sign showed that they were still ten miles from Clints Well.

"Strategy," Kitty said as soon as she sat in the car. "What exactly do you suggest we do in this next village?"

"Find the truck."

"How?"

"How would you do it, KGB expert?"

"That would depend on how big the town is."

"My guess is a filling station, five stores and about twenty houses. We'll have to wait and see."

"Then we casually ask questions about the semi and trailer."

"Sounds reasonable. How did you get this far tracking Dunning?"

She looked at him a moment and shrugged. "We watched his apartment in Houston. He left hurriedly one morning, and we lost him in traffic. We returned to his apartment, questioned the cleaning lady thoroughly, and we found some old letters and trash that led us to Winslow."

"And the cleaning lady?"

"She. . .she had an accident."

"With Niki's help, I'll bet." Bolan's mouth tightened. For a long moment he wanted to break his word and not cooperate with this killer. He wanted to lash out, to make Kitty look the same way April Rose had—so still, so limp, so forever taken away from him. The Executioner gripped the wheel tightly, and then the emotional surge was past.

He glanced at her as he drove and she nodded.

"Again I think you made the right decision just now, about continuing to cooperate," she said. "Our work must always be on a nonpersonal basis, and it cannot take into account our private lives. We should think only of our governments.''

Bolan started to say something, then decided against it. First he would find Dunning, then he would deal with the KGB.

Clints Well was a small village. There were only two stores, a filling station and twenty-odd vacation cabins scattered in the hills. Bolan parked in front of the general store. He'd seen many just like it in some of the smallest towns and crossroads of the country. And in the best tradition, this one had an overhanging porch to shield those on the boardwalk. Six wooden chairs sat lined up against the front wall, and three were occupied by the town's old-timers. Bolan figured they would be the best information source in the county.

''Let's split up. That tractor trailer would stand out like a stagecoach here. I'll take the old-timers. See you back here in ten minutes.''

Kitty nodded, gripped her purse with the strap securely over the shoulder and entered the general store.

Bolan climbed the steps and pointed to the empty chair next to one of the men. The old-timer, whom Bolan guessed to be about seventy, touched the peak of his railroad cap with one finger and shrugged. The Executioner sat down, leaned the chair back against the wall, then folded his hands on his chest and relaxed.

Five minutes later the old man beside Bolan, sighed. ''Goin' far?''

''Nope.''

''Wife buying some stuff, I guess?''

''Likely.''

''Not a big talker, are you?''

''Not usually.''

''You lost?''

"Do I look lost?"

"Yes. And a stranger. We don't get many strangers here on purpose. Had one yesterday. Trying to find Phoenix."

"I'm not lost, but I did lose something up here. A truck."

"That so?" the second old man asked.

"True. Big highway diesel with a thirty-foot trailer."

"Hard rig to lose."

"Somebody hijacked it."

"Figures. Worth a lot. You say it was a Jimmy or a Reo?"

"Nope. A Kenworth. You see one the past few days?"

"Yep. Logging rig, lots of log trucks up here. South-west Logging Company kills a lot of ponderosa pine hereabouts."

Bolan played the waiting game.

"You see a Kenworth with a thirty-foot trailer?" Bolan asked.

"Yep."

"Red paint job?" Bolan asked.

"Nope, a sissy-green. But mebbe the hijacker had her repainted."

"She still around?"

"Not by a damn sight. Our deputy sheriff gave the sucker a ticket for illegal parking. Cost him forty-five bucks plus twenty costs. Guy driving her made a lot of noise about us having a ticket trap in a nothing town. Said they never did this over in Pine. That cost him a hundred for contempt. After that he ramrodded that rig out of town and almost got himself a speeding ticket. Biggest damn case we had here in three, four months."

"Was the driver a Japanese with a flattop haircut?"

"Well, now. How did you know that? Yessiree, he was. And he lit out screaming that he was glad to be out of our town."

Bolan let the chair fall forward on all four legs. He stood slowly and stretched. "I better move over toward Pine. That little Oriental is going to get himself in a lot more trouble. Thanks, men, for your help."

The old men smiled. The blue eyes of the first one were half clouded by a growing white film. "Young feller, you just more than welcome. You drive safe and come back and see us sometime, y'hear?"

The hint of a smile touched Bolan's mouth. It would be good to sit there on the boardwalk, chair tipped back against the wall and watch the world go by.

Yeah.

7

Mack Bolan wondered why it all had been so easy as he lay in the grass of a high-country valley and looked through light timber at a thirty-foot aluminum trailer at the edge of the campground.

He and Kitty had driven the twenty miles to Pine, which had over a thousand year-round residents and in the summer three times that many. The Japanese man, his semi and thirty-foot trailer had stopped in the town's two biggest gas stations and asked the same question. He wanted diesel fuel and wanted to find a local campground. In each station he got into an argument with the workers. At one place it almost ended in a fight. Everyone remembered the guy with the green Kenworth and the big trailer.

Both times the attendants told Yamaguchi where the camp called Pine Valley was located, about a mile on out the highway and below the Mogolion Rim.

Bolan studied the trailer again, then signaled for Kitty to stay down, and he ran another twenty yards forward through the timber and faded behind a tall tree. The trailer sat just ahead at the end of a private campground.

There was only one other camper, a tent at the far end, a quarter of a mile away. The tractor was nowhere in sight. Bolan saw no activity around the trailer. A set of steps stood at the rear of the rig, and the back door was closed.

He lifted the Ingram and charged toward the goal, this time moving thirty yards. He hit a trip wire just before he made it to his target pine. When he realized what he had done, he dived and rolled to the tree, protecting the submachine gun against his gut.

Five seconds after he kicked the wire, a mind-jarring explosion tore through the silence of the high pine country, blasting a hole in the stillness.

Bolan pushed his forehead into the pine needles as he listened for the singing of shrapnel from the blast, but there was none. Strange. He was not even scratched.

The Executioner ran again toward the trailer. This time he didn't feel the thin copper wire break as his foot rammed through it. The strand of metal let fall a half-pound weight that activated a spring, which in turn pulled the trigger back on an M-16 automatic rifle fifteen yards from Bolan. The weapon fired straight up into the air until the 20-round magazine went dry.

He looked behind and saw Kitty running forward, her Luger up and ready as she darted from tree to tree.

The trailer was in plain view now, less than thirty yards ahead. The Executioner did not like the situation. Where had the opposition come from? The trip wire he had hit would be a first warning. He guessed the explosion had been concussion grenades or perhaps two sticks of dynamite hung in a tree with something to trigger them. But the M-16. Who would fire twenty rounds from an M-16 without stopping?

It had to be something mechanical. A setup.

Another defensive, manless setup. Bolan snorted as he got up and raced toward the rear of the trailer. He made it with no more traps, no more shooting or explosions. He flipped the handle on the tall half door and jerked it open.

"Don't shoot! Please, don't shoot, mister!"

Bolan lowered the Ingram. The man inside the trailer sat in a chair beside a card table. He was about twenty. He had a radio, a big ice chest, a twenty-four-bottle carton of Coca-Cola and a box filled with food. On the table was a partly finished jigsaw puzzle. Otherwise the trailer was empty.

"What was all that noise out there?" he asked.

Bolan leaned against the tailgate of the trailer. He shook his head and looked at Kitty, who had just come up beside him. "He's done it again. This was all a false lead to throw us off his trail and buy him time."

Ten minutes later, Bolan had it all spelled out.

"So this little Oriental guy with the strange flat haircut asked me if I wanted to make a hundred dollars," the young man was explaining. Bolan and Kitty stood at the end of the trailer drinking Cokes from the kid's supply. He wore cutoff jeans and no shirt. A straw hat lay on the floor beside his worn sneakers.

The youth looked at Kitty. "Miss, I've been out of work. Do you know how long it's been since I made a whole hundred dollars all by myself?"

"And this gentleman said all you had to do was sit in the trailer for three days, as a kind of secret guard?" Kitty asked.

"Yes, ma'am. So I will. Got me all the comforts of home. Unless I'm doing something illegal."

"Not as far as I know," Bolan said. "We understand. About the noise outside, it looked to me like it was some campers using up their leftover Fourth of July fireworks."

AN HOUR LATER Kitty and Bolan were back in Clints Well. Kitty looked over at Bolan.

"Do you never get tired? You said you had driven all night last night. How long has it been since you have had any sleep?"

"Couple of days. I can sleep after we've found Dunning."

"You try that for too long and we may never sleep again. There is no motel within thirty-five miles of here. We can sleep in the car."

"You take a nap. I want to buy my friends up here a beer."

"I can work if you can. So Dunning planted that bogus trailer on us, and the driver caused trouble so everyone would remember him. Where did the real trailer go?"

"Must be around here somewhere. All we have to do is find it."

"And you think the old men might know?"

"Yeah."

As usual with a July day in the high country of Arizona, the thunderheads had been building up all morning, and now lightning flashed as a thunderstorm powered across the land. The rain dimpled the dusty areas, splashed the Ford's windshield and washed off the mountain.

"It won't last long," Bolan said. "The natives say this happens every day this time of year."

It was a fast-moving shower that lasted only four minutes. Bolan opened the door.

"I'll be back soon," he said and ran for the porch overhang in front of the general store. This time there were only two grandfather types in the loafers' chairs. One of them was the man Bolan had talked to earlier that afternoon.

The Executioner sat down next to the old man in the

faded blue overalls and rocked back, closed his eyes and took a long breath.

"You find that sucker?" the old man asked.

"Uh-huh."

"So why you back here?"

"Wrong trailer. My little buddy bushwhacked us. You saw the one he wanted you to see. 'Pears he was through here a day or two before that with another trailer, one he slid through so quiet you couldn't hear them diesel valves clicking."

"How you know that, young feller?"

"Figures. The one we found was empty."

The old man laughed. "He tricked you. Now you wanting to know, did we see that tractor with a look-alike trailer a day or so before the big traffic ticket affair. I reckon we did, yes."

Bolan nodded and looked away. "Could I buy you gents a beer?"

"Nope, but a cold Pepsi would go good for Will and me."

Bolan went into the store and came back with three iced colas. Both the older men drank, smacked their lips and held the cold cans against their cheeks.

"Well, 'pears we got to tell you, bribing us this-a-ways." The loafers laughed and Bolan joined in.

"See, first time the green Kenworth came through we wondered about her. Slid in about dusk, tooled past, and then we could see her turn off down McCollough Lane. That's maybe two miles north of town, but we could follow her lights all the way. Those big Christmas-tree lights showed up just plain. Then she turned and the clearance lights blinked out, so we knew she was in the ponderosa down there. The only road that turns off is McCollough Lane, and the only place that goes is back into the woods and to some forestry gates. All National Forest in there, of course.''

''Couple of miles to the lane,'' Bolan said. ''You sure?''

''Yessir, damn sure. We couldn't figure out what a rig like that would be doing heading back on that lane. Trailer looked the same when we seen it the next day. We just figured the driver got himself good and lost and then came back to town. He stopped here and asked directions and got his ass arrested, then he drove on out to Pine way we told. He had to come back here to go to Pine.''

Bolan finished his can of Pepsi and handed the empty to the old man. ''That's worth a nickel deposit in Oregon next time you go through. Thanks for the help.'' Bolan walked away.

''Damn big-city spenders think they can stomp all over us country folk,'' the old man said. He laughed and winked with his one good eye.

A short time later, Bolan drove down McCollough Lane for a mile before he pulled the Ford into a side trail and hid it behind some brush and towering piñon and ponderosa pine trees. It was almost dark. They had a conference and decided Kitty would sleep in the car.

Bolan stood for a moment behind the car with the blanket.

Bolan waved and vanished into the light brush. He settled down in a thicket for concealment and went to sleep almost at once.

8

"Sam, your only job is to monitor the power-input cycle board. I want you to tell me if it varies so much as a flutter off the mark on this digital readout. Without the proper voltage and cycle, my whole operation can be off a mile." Dr. Dunning gave Sam a wave of approval and turned back to his large main console.

Six CRT screens showed him readouts; dozens of dials and digital displays had been arranged in related order and grouped around him. He snapped on six toggle switches and watched the boards light up.

Dr. Dunning typed a simple command into the computer keyboard: "Track identified orbiter." Then he sat back and waited. The readouts told him the target was soon coming around the earth on its regular orbiting pass.

When it arrived, he deftly locked his tracer onto target, and punched up new instructions to his computer: "Send first batch of access codes to the targeted orbiter on its frequency."

Dr. Dunning stood, walked around the chair and sat down. Usually there was someone to talk to, to worry with at a time like this when there was nothing left to do but wait and hope. Now he was alone.

Sam did not seem to care what was happening. The forty thousand potential coded words were sent within seconds, and then he waited for three minutes. That was plenty of time. The codes had not broken through the security system of the orbiter for capture. He ordered the second batch of forty thousand codes transmitted. Again he paced for three minutes.

Nothing happened. He had not gained control to the on-board computer of the orbiter. Again he sent out a new batch of codes he had determined might be used for capture.

Weeks ago he had given his computer a few basic codes he judged might be used by the Russian orbiter for its access. He then instructed the computer to work out every possible variable of the basic combinations he had sent, stopping at 1.5 million. The computer worked out the code variables, grouped them in batches of forty thousand, and stored them in memory. There were 37.5 batches of codes.

Ten times Dr. Dunning sent out the potential code access words, and ten times the screens in front of him remained blank.

He had not broken the orbiter's secret. The vehicle had now passed over the U.S. on its continuing orbit, and he would no longer try for capture.

Dr. Dunning shrugged. Trial and error. Often it took many attempts to break an access code. He might not win with his first 1.5 million tries. If so, he would put the computer to work expanding other possible codes utilizing new words, names and numbers.

One and a half hours after the first try, he gained a tracking report from his antenna as the vehicle came around on the next orbit. He locked onto the vehicle and tried again.

On the third batch of codes he sent, the voltage fell off.

"Dammit, Sam! Get the voltage back up there. Push it!"

Dr. Dunning was not a swearing man. He saw the voltage level come up and stabilize, and he waited for results.

Sam had looked up in surprise, and his face showed a flash of anger before he pushed the lever and adjusted the buttons as Dr. Dunning had instructed him.

The ex-NASA scientist looked back at his gauges and relaxed.

A minute later the center screen flashed on. He had the right code. The orbiter was asking for instructions. *He had capture!*

At once he punched up the correct commands on the keyboard in front of him. The plain language was translated into telemetric signals and shot at the orbiter as fast as Dr. Dunning could type them in. He consulted a pad and copied the elaborate system of commands he had worked out for the orbiter. Then he sent a new command that would change the access code in the orbiter's computer. The new code contained three illogical and unrelated elements. Dr. Dunning figured there would be only one chance in a billion that any computer could break his code. He sent the new coding instructions and leaned back.

There had been two new basic commands given the orbiter. One was to change its orbit line by ten degrees. That would be enough to alert its owners that something had changed. The second order was to cease all transmissions except those specifically asked for by the new ground base.

Dr. Dunning smiled as he watched the data being sent out and received and absorbed. He now *owned* that space vehicle up there.

"You can relax, Sam. We have capture! We are now the proud new fathers of an orbiter slamming around the earth at just under seventeen thousand miles an hour at an altitude of twenty-two thousand miles. Congratulations!"

Sam smiled. Dr. Dunning could not remember many smiles on the face of the young Oriental.

"It's you who is to be congratulated, Dr. Dunning. You have done what other smaller men only dream of doing. This means that you will go down in history."

IT WAS 5:30 A.M. in Washington, D.C. An aide hurried through a silent wing of the White House and knocked softly on a solid door. He opened it cautiously and strode into the bedroom of the President of the United States.

The form under the sheet came alert at once and sat up.

"Mr. President, I'm sorry to bother you. But the hot line has been activated. It's the Premier. It seems that we have some kind of a major problem facing us."

"You mean they've found out?" The President pulled on a robe and slippers and walked down the deserted corridor to his Oval Office.

"Has Harloff been alerted?"

The aide nodded. "He's waiting in there, sir."

Inside the President's office stood four men, all with serious expressions. An unshaven young man in a T-shirt and pajama pants stood beside the President's desk holding the red phone which usually was locked in a side drawer. The young man's age and appearance belied the strength, maturity and conviction that were revealed when he spoke.

"Mr. President, I'll translate as usual. Try to pick up the tone and inflection of the Premier's voice if you can. It is just after lunchtime in Moscow. The Premier's aide has been talking with a controlled fury. I think this is a complaint of a high order.'' He handed the President the red phone and picked up the blue handset.

Harloff knew that on the other end the Russian Premier and his translator were in a similar mode. It was now a four-way conference call. Harloff would listen to the Russian translation of what the President said and confirm the content. The Russian translator in Moscow would listen to Harloff's Russian translation into English, and he would confirm it as proper.

"Mr. President, this is the Premier. I am outraged! I am surprised and shocked and terribly angry. How could you do such a thing? How could you threaten the world in this way?''

"Good evening, Mr. Premier. Before I can tell you if we did anything, I'll have to know what you are talking about. None of us here is aware of any international problem of any great significance.''

"Do not toy with me! You know perfectly well that your scientists, your space agency, have captured one of our orbiting satellites. You know this.''

"Mr. Premier, I did not know that you had lost a satellite.'' He looked at Gregory, his NASA chief, who had been summoned as usual with any activation of the hot line. The chief sent an aide running from the room. He shook his head at the President and gave him a note that said, "We know of no loss of any satellite. We did not, repeat did *not* capture one of theirs.''

"Our space agency knows nothing about any of your satellites that are missing, Mr. Premier. This is all a total surprise to us.''

There was a moment of muffled sounds from the other end after the translation was made, as if the Premier was conferring.

"Mr. President, we have never lied to each other before. I hope you are not doing so now."

"Mr. Premier, I speak the truth. I have given no orders and approved no orders to interfere in any way with any orbiting or space vehicles of any nation. I will not do so. My chief of NASA has given no such order, nor would he permit any such action without an order from me personally. I can assure you, Mr. Premier, if one of your pieces of space hardware is lost or strayed, it is not due to any action, forces, men or agents of the United States government."

After the translation there was a long pause.

"Mr. President, you do sound sincere, but we have facts that must be considered. The satellite was captured while out of our contact while over the United States. It was captured by breaking a secret access code, a highly difficult and technical problem in itself that only a world power would have the resources and facilities to undertake. And once the satellite was captured, its orbit was changed to make sure we knew it had been captured. We now cannot contact our own space vehicle. It must have been your space agency that did it, and they will not tell you."

After the translation there was a silence in the Oval Office. Fred Gregory shook his head emphatically. "Mr. President, we have not even thought of capturing a Russian satellite. We have not tried to. We have not captured. Period."

"Mr. Premier, we will check every possible explanation for your loss. But I am not optimistic. Our NASA people say they have not tried to capture, nor have they completed any capture of any orbiter. Perhaps it broke up or collided with another satellite. Maybe it was the French. They have been progressing with a more sophisticated telemetry."

"No, the French are not technically capable. Mr. President, it must have been your people. Some extreme fringe, some rebel, perhaps. Find out. We will allow you six hours to interrogate your NASA experts. If we do not receive some satisfactory explanation and return the craft, we will begin destroying one of your orbiting vehicles every six hours, until you admit your complicity and return the craft. We will expect a contact from you on this phone in exactly six hours. Goodbye, Mr. President."

The President of the United States had been standing by his executive chair, and as Harloff finished the translation and they heard a *"Da,"* from the other end confirming the correctness of the translation, he put the phone back on the red cradle.

"Six hours. I wonder what they lost? Fred, check known Soviet orbiters and find one with an orbit change last night. First we find out what they lost and then why. Hell, only six hours. It must be something important. Not just a weather or spy satellite. Check the big stuff. We know everything they have up there, and they know what we have. Everything. We better get moving. We have only six hours to come up with something."

9

Mack Bolan shifted his position on the soft forest mulch of a thousand years of pine needles and leaves. Then, with the darting quickness of a hummingbird changing directions, he was back in Stony Man Farm, Virginia. Security had been breached. They were under attack! Desperate men were trying to kill Colonel John Phoenix!

"No, no, dammit, over here! Shoot at me you sons of bitches! Not at anyone else, shoot at me. Don't fire at Kurtzman—he's not a combat soldier. Bear is hit—he's down!" Bolan jumped up and ran. It seemed the faster he moved, the distance to his computer wizard only increased. He could not help Kurtzman, who was down and hit badly. Bolan hosed the enemy with his M-16. He picked up his AutoMag triggering the .44 again and again at the man shadows charging across the blazing Virginia hellground.

Then someone came to help. A fine person, his own true love. She ran out, distracting the enemy, putting herself in the line of fire for him.

It could not be permitted to happen!

Sweet heaven, it simply could not happen! But he watched helplessly as the singing bullets slammed into her body, throwing her one way, blasting her back the other. He saw her hand reaching out to him, saw it stained blood red as her life substance drained out of her.

No! No! He leaped up and began to run at them, firing and running and shooting again. He never ran out of ammunition as he kept charging and blasting at the menacing faces that sprang at him from every shadow.

He uttered a long wailing cry of torment and anguish into the sky: "No, dammit to hell, it can't happen!"

Mack Bolan shook his head to clear it and sat up to find himself back in the pine forest high over Clints Well, Arizona. He was sure he had shouted the last line of his nightmare into the darkness. The sound of his own voice had wakened him. He sat there, crouched low, listening to the night sounds.

Had anyone heard? Had he actually shouted aloud? The Executioner wiped sweat off his forehead and held the Ingram ready. It was on automatic mode and held a full magazine.

Slowly he relaxed and eased his finger from the trigger.

Bolan shivered and lay down, drawing the blanket around him in the chill of the seven-thousand-foot mountain elevation.

He looked at his watch. It was 3:00 A.M. Sleep would come again, but no more dreams. He willed his mind not to dream.

Soon he slept again and he did not dream.

Mack Bolan woke up, stretched and worked out a few stiff joints from the chill of the Arizona highlands. He pushed the Ingram to one side on the cord around his neck and carried the folded blanket toward the car.

Nothing warned him.

It was the combat awareness, sharpness of years of being a fugitive and staying alive, that saved him. He paused fifty yards from the car and observed through the trees. Everything looked peaceful enough.

Kitty was up and leaning against the fender of the car, combing her hair. She wore jeans and a blouse. The car radio had been turned on and a newscast was just ending.

It looked normal, but it was all wrong. She did not have her purse and her Luger with her. Kitty never left her gun far from her reach. She kept glancing to her left at a thick stand of brush. A Phoenix news station was broadcasting local news. Bolan ignored it. His combat-trained eyes dissected every part of the scene around the car and Kitty.

Movement.

Where? It had been in his peripheral vision. Bolan swept the scene again. The brush that Kitty had glanced at wavered. There was no wind yet. Bolan concentrated on the shape, form and shadows of the brush spot ten feet in front of the car. It moved again.

Company. One concealed ambusher was in the scrub. Again Bolan scanned the area around the car, not looking selectively as the eye usually does, but looking at the whole scene at once, like a camera. Closer to him he found the second man in a position where he could get a good cross fire on a target at the front of the car without endangering Kitty.

The Executioner moved silently through the forty yards toward his first suspect. Not a leaf stirred in the early dawn. No birds were out. It was limbo time between the night creatures and the daywalkers. That meant no covering sound. Music came on the radio as Kitty moved to the door and turned up the volume. Thanks, Kitty.

Bolan edged around a ponderosa and spotted the figure twenty feet ahead. He wore camouflaged Army clothes. He was small and when he turned, checking to each side, Bolan saw that he was Japanese and had a flattop haircut. Strange that he should be here. Bolan wished he had brought the silenced Beretta. No, the man was still an innocent. The Executioner spotted the Oriental's weapon, a deadly black M-16 automatic rifle held loosely, confidently. Strike one.

Bolan checked his own pockets. Nothing to rattle or clink. No coins or keys. He stood silently, moved like a grounded wisp of fog to the next tree and paused. Now he would be exposed if his target in front of him turned. Bolan fisted the Ingram, put it on automatic fire and stepped forward, cat quiet. The mark turned and looked left, but not behind him. Bolan froze to stay out of the man's side vision. The guard turned back to watch Kitty.

Bolan took two more quick steps and knelt beside the Japanese before he sensed someone was near. When he jerked his head around, Bolan pressed the muzzle of the Ingram against the man's lips.

"One sound and you're dead," Bolan whispered. The man nodded. "How many of you here?"

The guard moved one hand slowly and held up one finger. Bolan pushed the barrel into his mouth. Beads of sweat popped out on the gunner's forehead. He held up two fingers. Bolan withdrew the barrel.

"Who are you working for?"

"Yamaguchi."

"Why didn't you kill her and then wait for me?"

"Yamaguchi said no killing down this far. Too messy. We just capture whoever shows up and hold them for three days."

Suddenly Bolan surged on top of the supine man, pinning his hands to his chest, then Bolan's trained thumbs found the carotid arteries on each side of the guard's throat and pressed. Twenty seconds later the Japanese was unconscious.

Bolan shackled the man's wrists and ankles with police plastic riot cuffs. The only way to get them off was to cut them free. The guard would be unconscious for ten minutes, which should be long enough.

Bolan crawled back into the heavier brush and timber and circled the site, moving within twenty feet of the other ambusher, who also was Japanese with a flattop haircut and wore camouflage fatigues. No wonder Yamaguchi could be in two places at one time. He had clones.

Bolan flipped the Ingram to automatic fire and stood.

"Hey there, friend," he said. The surprised soldier on the ground turned sharply, saw the submachine gun aimed at him and wilted.

"Don't even breathe. One sound and your next meal is hot lead."

The gunman nodded. Bolan moved up and fastened the man's wrists behind him, then marched him to the car where Kitty still stood.

"Glad to see you, Mack."

"I'll bet you are. They caught you sleeping?"

"Yes, but it will be the last time."

"It almost was, for you," the captive said. Bolan turned to the Japanese and backhanded him across the mouth.

"Now, tell us what this little war game is all about."

"I was out deer hunting."

Bolan slammed the edge of a stiffened palm into the side of the man's neck, driving him to his knees. It was not hard enough to break his neck, but would leave a painful bruise for days.

"We're not law-enforcement officers. So don't try

your kid hoodlum chatter with us. Answer the questions and you just may survive the next five minutes.''

The man's eyes widened, he nodded and stood slowly.

"Hey, take it easy! Okay, we're friends of Yamaguchi's. He's got this little organization. Most of us are in the reserve National Guard with him. He says he's got an operation going here that is bigger than anything we ever dreamed of. That's all we know. He says stay here and stop anyone from coming up the road. We stop them.''

"You didn't ask Yamaguchi why?''

"You don't ask Yamaguchi anything.''

"I will. How far up this road is the trailer?''

"He didn't tell us. We've never been up the road.''

"How many men does Yamaguchi have in his whole operation?''

"I don't know. I've seen twenty of us from the Guard but he's talked about thirty men. I don't know.''

"Anything else to tell us?''

The man shook his head.

"Fine.'' Bolan slashed a karate blow into the side of his neck and then another as the man was going down, plunging him into dreamland. Then he bound the man's wrists with plastic binders.

"I am sorry, Mack. They caught me changing clothes and I could not get to my purse. They were here waiting for me when I woke up. I . . . .''

Bolan held up his hand. "Forget it. Just a slight delay, and we picked up some intel.'' He grabbed the Japanese and carried him into the brush beside the first one. Let them suffer together when they came to.

Bolan considered using the car, but rejected the idea. He went to his weapons case and took out some aid and comfort. He decided to change into his black skinsuit.

Kitty watched him.

"What in the world is that thing?"

"My working clothes—hard to see at night."

Kitty shrugged and looked through one of her suit-cases and took out a weapon, a German-made Schmeisser MP-40 submachine gun.

Bolan slid into the skinsuit, filled the slit pockets with equipment he would need and put on his combat webbing, added four grenades and his Colt Commander in the holster. The Executioner took some C-4 primer cord, two quarter-pound chunks of C-4 plastic explosive and six extra magazines for the Ingram. He checked the pouches on the web belt and saw that all were filled. Then he strapped the Childers battle shotgun on his back.

Bolan left the car where it was parked off the road and out of sight. They walked back to the forestry trail, keeping twenty yards into the tall pine country and its light cover of brush.

Bolan approved Kitty's new costume, the tight blue jeans and blue bouse. She also wore sturdy hiking boots and now slid in a magazine and charged the MP-40. She said she had four more magazines in her shoulder purse.

They moved slowly, carefully, alert for trip wires and any kind of warning devices. Bolan did not expect much, figuring the first security would be five miles from the trailer. Nearly a mile up the road they came to a gate across the trail.

Heavy timber at this point prevented any four-wheelers from driving around the gate. Bolan checked the padlock and chain on the metal barrier. The lock was shiny new, the chain was old and showed signs of nicks and burrs. The old lock had been cut off. On the far side of the gate he found heavy truck tire tracks.

They were the same as the ones he had been following up the road. They were still on the right trail.

A hundred yards farther along, Bolan sensed the trap. It was his old combat awareness, that sixth sense that separates the natural combatmen from the wounded and dying.

"Get down!" Bolan thundered, diving at Kitty and knocking her off her feet. They both rolled behind a large fallen log just as the space where they had stood was riddled by twenty rounds from two or three M-16s.

Bolan's eyes were angry. "Those weren't rounds from Dr. Dunning's set guns. Those were live riflemen trying to kill us right here. Somehow every rule in the old book has been changed. It's now kill or be killed."

Kitty lay behind the log, her face drawn as she rubbed her elbow where it had hit a rock.

"How many of them?" she asked.

"Two, maybe three. You stay here. I'll go around. . . ." He stopped when her expression changed.

"No, Mack. My turn. You stay here and cover me as I swing around behind them. I have done this before."

Bolan nodded, lifted his Ingram and sent a dozen rounds from his chatter gun into the woods ahead of them. He had no target, but it would give them something to think about. He fired again, watched Kitty slip beyond the fallen trunk, and then he rose and squeezed off another 5-round burst.

He crawled ten feet along the ground and fired again. This time he kept on moving. It was no time to leave his fate in the hands of the KGB. This one agent of theirs might help him, but he was damned if he was going to rely on her for anything!

Bolan paused at the end of the log, dashed to the first tree, then the second. No one fired at him. He darted for the third and felt the slug before he heard the sound of the M-16. The burning bullet creased his right thigh and kept on going as Bolan dived toward the nearest cover. He hit on one shoulder, executed a roll and kept turning trying to get out of the open space. There was no option—he had to be hidden before the gunman refined his sight for the next shot.

10

It was twenty-four seconds after midnight in Moscow. The Premier of the Union of Soviet Socialist Republics had just finished talking with the President of the United States of America. Most of the Premier's advisors were still in the room when a glow outside his window caught the group's attention. At once it changed into a brilliant flash that shattered the darkness with a continuing dazzling light much like noontime. They all rushed to the window and found that it was daylight all over Moscow.

Twenty-five thousand miles above Moscow, a hydrogen warhead had been detonated. The blinding flash moderated into bright sunshine by the time it penetrated the gloom on the night side of the planet Earth. The spurious daylight set roosters crowing, sent owls scooting for their daytime perches and turned off millions of photosensitive street lights.

The Premier staggered back, fearing another blast would follow, that Armageddon had indeed come to the world. But within seconds, two of his advisors assured him that there had been no report of incoming missiles. Quickly they determined that the explosion had been hydrogen and had been thousands of miles above the earth.

Five minutes later reports began streaming in. It was confirmed that the explosion was twenty-five thousand miles high, exactly over Moscow.

"Was it one of ours?" the Premier asked his defense chief.

"We have no way of knowing. We realize what is missing. It is possible, but we should hope for the best. It would be my suggestion that we postpone any overt action against American satellites until this new mystery is solved."

The Premier nodded, watching the light continue outside. He had no idea how long it would remain, how much noon at midnight they would have. But even as he watched, the light began to fade. Ten minutes. The power! What massive power had been released!

"We will not phone the President. It is four in the afternoon there. We shall wait until it is our daytime and their night when we talk again."

EIGHT HOURS LATER, at precisely twelve midnight, Washington, D.C. time, a similar explosion took place twenty-five thousand miles above the capital. There was a hushed reaction in the President's Oval Office.

The Chief Executive and his advisors had been meeting since four that afternoon trying to decide what had caused the brilliant explosion over Moscow as reported by observers in many European countries.

They knew the altitude and had followed reports of possible radiation levels in the upper atmosphere, which most now thought would be negligible.

The President shielded his eyes as he watched the rose garden come into full view and then turn garish in the harsh overlighting. He stood at the window, sure that there would be no nuclear explosion. Knowing that it was not the forerunner of a thermonuclear holocaust, he was still amazed.

"Why?" The President threw the challenge at his advisors.

Secretary of Defense Jensen held up his hands. "We simply don't know. One over Moscow, one here. Where else? We don't have anything but speculation. The Third World might be making a spectacular display of its new nuclear capability, and tomorrow they may demand parity in all things—all wealth, all development—otherwise we will feel the might of their weapons at five thousand feet. Nobody knows what the hell is going on."

"Find out!" snapped the president. "I want to know everything I can when I talk to the Premier in the morning."

He waved his hand and everyone but his legal advisor, the man some called the presidential clone, left the office at once.

"This could be disastrous," the President said. "By tomorrow morning I want to know exactly what is happening, and if the theft of that Russian 'orbiter' has anything to do with it. If the Reds lost what they might have lost, the whole thing would be much simpler. But that's almost too much to hope for. Get on those guys out there. Make them produce. Notify me up if anything else big breaks."

THREE HOURS LATER, at precisely midnight in Oregon, a radio signal turned on a powerful transmitter on a peak in the Mount Hood National Forest six miles from the nearest road. A rather stiff, nonprofessional voice spilled into thousands of Oregon and Washington late-night listeners' ears, overriding the normal program signals, booming over rock and roll, country, Top 40 and talk-show stations alike. The voice gave a clear and persuasive narrative about what had happened over Moscow and then over Washington, D.C.

Newsmen rolled out of bed. Front pages were scrapped and remade. Radio and TV broadcasts were shuffled and rewritten. The voices came on again, repeating the fifteen-minute description of events and then degenerated into a diatribe for world peace and disarmament of offensive weapons.

"Good morning from the Pacific Northwest. This is radio station TRUE reporting on the world events of the day. At exactly midnight in Washington, D.C., and eight hours earlier, at midnight, over Moscow, hydrogen missile warheads were detonated. There is no danger and no damage. The missiles that carried the warheads were detonated at twenty-five thousand miles in space, and created a daylike period of ten to twelve minutes in both capitals. The explosions caused a certain amount of panic, but there was no loss of life or structural damage in either city.

"I captured the missiles that resulted in the explosions. They are both intended to be a warning to the world: don't let the big powers kill our planet by launching a nuclear war. Both the United States and Russia are more dangerously close to such a blunder right now than either nation realizes.

"The two MIRV warheads that exploded came from a Russian missile orbiting the earth. This Russian supermissile was loaded with twenty-four independently targetable warheads. Each has the power of the two that were exploded last night. All are hydrogen bombs, all are monstrously deadly. The twenty-four warheads on this one vehicle are not alone in outer space.

"Russia has twelve such vehicles now in orbit around the earth, flying directly over your house, threatening every human being in the world. That means Russia still controls two hundred eighty-six independently targeted hydrogen bombs ready to drop on your home at any instant!

"MIRV is an acronym for Multiple Independently targetable Re-entry Vehicle.

"A few hours ago I electronically captured one Russian missile. I'm sure they burned up the hot line to Washington trying to get it back from the President, without telling him what the vehicle actually was. These weapons are in space in spite of an agreement that space should be free of all weapons, especially the MIRV type. Both the U.S. and Russia agreed to such an agreement.

"My name is Dr. Peter Dunning. I worked for NASA for many years, and while there I actively campaigned for a reduction in offensive weapons and a reliance on defensive ones such as countermissiles and defensive screens. Soon I became counterproductive to NASA, so I resigned.

"It permitted me time to work on my own project: to capture a Russian MIRV missile to prove to the world how the big powers lie to us; how they endanger us; how they threaten us with hydrogen war if we don't do just as they say. I captured the Russian Armageddon device on my own, without the help or the knowledge of the U.S. government or the space administration.

"They would have stopped me. It is my purpose to ban all nuclear weapons from outer space. You will hear more from me soon. Let me tell you why I am doing all this."

AT HIS DESK IN PORTLAND, OREGON, the night monitor on the Federal Communications Commission took a phone call from his regional boss. It was 1:15 A.M.

"Heard it yet?"

"Heard what?"

"The pirate broadcasting on three frequencies. He's

blasting half the Portland stations off the air. What are you monitoring anyway? Get moving on it now. Highest priority. I just had a call from Washington, D.C., and this is hot. Get our pilot and our aerial triangulation team set up for takeoff at dawn from Troutdale airport. We have to find this outlaw an hour after daybreak or it's our asses!''

The night man spun dials until he picked up the illegal broadcast. He rushed to the roof of the building and set up the portable direction antenna. Five minutes later he had a sighting line drawn on his map. It went nearly due east from Portland, passing directly over the summit of Mount Hood.

The longer he looked at the line, the more he realized that the pirate was going to be out there in the middle of the Mount Hood National Forest, somewhere so inaccessible that they would have to hike in ten miles to find it. No. He made another phone call. There would be a chopper loaded and ready at the Troutdale airport at dawn.

Once they were in the air they could work a quick triangulation and pin down the approximate position. Then another cross from ten miles away and they could pinpoint that transmitter and have the chopper over the spot in less than four minutes. He set his jaw grimly and turned back to the illegal broadcast.

''There is no place in a peaceful world for the threat of a holocaust to be whispering overhead every waking hour. The twelve vehicles are now in orbit, circling the earth every ninety-four minutes. They are spaced apart and on different orbits, with primary target in the U.S. and Western Europe already coded and ready for firing. These warheads can hit any place on earth, can come smashing down out of orbit from almost straight overhead, giving practically no early-warning time.

"Some experts say that a properly launched orbiting missile can be exploding at ten thousand feet over a radar antenna, at the exact instant that such an early warning radar picks up its first notice of a potential danger. In other words, zero warning time! Do you want to live with that monster over your living room, watching your baby go to sleep, following your teen-agers on a picnic?

"This is a warning to all nations with atomic weapons. The owners of such armaments from missiles to bombs to satchel charges to artillery shells will be destroyed soon. Contact your government representatives today to support me. Urge total disarmament now, before it is too late!"

The air was silent for a moment, then the broadcast began again, repeating itself on the looped tape in the small tape recorder-player.

At the Troutdale airport just before dawn, the Federal Communications chopper warmed up, awaiting the last team member. He arrived, jumped in and it took off as soon as the door closed. They had everything they needed on board, and headed due east toward Mount Hood. They would check the first azimuth, then pivot at a ninety-degree angle to that one and take another reading on the broadcast. When they had three given azimuths they would draw the lines and have an exact target. It would be easy—there was no movement at all of the signal.

The chopper beat through the early-morning mists as the men inside worked with deliberate speed. They could not be wrong on this. The whole department could go down the tubes.

They would know in twenty minutes exactly where the transmitter was. They had to. There was no alternative.

11

The Executioner ended his roll into the forest floor, holding the submachine gun against his chest. He came to a stop behind a huge pine. Three more slugs pounded harmlessly into the piñon five seconds late. The shooter was somewhere in front of Bolan. He wondered where Kitty was. She had started to circle to the left.

Bolan peered around the trunk from the right side, saw movement ahead but was not sure who it was or the exact location. He crawled to the next tree four feet away, found he was in a shallow depression and scurried another twenty feet, moving around the suspected target. He came to his feet behind a ponderosa and looked around it.

At first he could see nothing unusual. He concentrated on a sturdy tree ahead that presented a good field of fire in front of it. The position would be a natural protection for a sniper position. Bolan watched for two minutes and at last saw a head poke out from the left side of the tree to scan the area.

The Executioner quickly picked out his new route to get to the side of the ambusher. He winced at the pain in his thigh, but knew it was a minor wound and ignored it. He fired a 4-round burst to the left of the target so the sniper would think he was safe. Then Bolan hurried for cover fifteen feet to the right and forward, starting to circle the enemy.

Bolan heard return fire, but it was aimed at his old position. He flattened behind a downed log and crawled to the front of it. He was far enough around now so he could see the sniper's legs spread out behind the tree. The man had not moved.

Bolan lifted the Ingram and sprayed ten shots at the camou-clad legs, and paused. The gunman wailed, spun around and started to return fire just as Bolan emptied the Ingram's magazine. The rounds slammed into the enemy's chest, pulping his aorta and slashing through his heart in a death surge that flung the bushwhacker to the side into sudden and everlasting death.

Bolan tensed and listened. Was there one gunner, two or more? He heard nothing for two minutes. He invested another sixty seconds in caution, then moved soundlessly toward the body. It lay sprawled on the forest floor. Bolan had put a new magazine in the Ingram and now paused at the side of a protective pine watching the area ahead. It was far too early to move in. Kitty must be up there somewhere. He could see the dead man plainly now. He was Japanese and had a flat-top haircut. The uniform.

Bolan waited again. There had to be more than one man on a roadblock like this. As Bolan watched the greenery, he saw movement. Another minute and he could make out someone coming through the trees, working toward the lifeless defender.

Another minute and he was sure it was Kitty. He wanted to yell at her to go back, but it was too late. She moved cautiously, but too soon. She held the submachine gun in front of her, ready. She ran the last dozen feet lightly, both hands on the gun, ready to fire. At the body she stopped, surveyed the area and was about to turn when Bolan saw someone else move. A man was behind her, deeper in the woods. Bolan tensed and swung the Ingram up. A few seconds later he spotted two men sliding from tree to tree, advancing on Kitty. Both were armed.

He waited until they were ten feet from her. It was obvious they were trying to capture her, not kill her. At ten feet they had an open spot to cross, and Bolan drilled the first charging man with a 10-round burst, splitting his chest and neck with a cascade of buzzing rounds that drove him backward into perpetual silence. The second man vanished into the brush.

"Kitty! Get down. There's another one," Bolan bellowed at the Russian agent. Then he ran in the direction the third defender had taken.

They could not afford to let anyone escape and alert Dr. Dunning of their presence. Bolan was still surprised by the shooting defense. He had figured more benign measures, not bullets and combat-trained defenders. These National Guard troops were no slouches.

The Executioner sprinted for fifty yards, then paused and listened. Ahead, he heard twigs cracking as he shifted course to the left. He could see little through the scrub cedar here. They were smaller and closer together, offering a good screen.

Bolan ran through them cautiously, watching ahead, careful not to rustle a leaf or break a dead branch. Again he paused. He was on the crest of a small slope, and the direction still seemed to be straight ahead. Bolan scanned the bushy area and saw a man twenty yards down the hill. The figure paused, breathing hard, and looked backward. Then he came to a path, turned right and began to jog along it.

Bolan checked the terrain. The trail led into a small ravine that worked upward toward a peak to the far right three or four miles away. Bolan turned more sharply right than the man had and ran through the sparser growth and down the hill to the right. He hoped to cut across the trail and wait for the runner.

The Executioner pushed faster, sacrificing a certain amount of stealth now to permit speed. Five minutes later he came to the faint trail and found an observation point where the path came straight at him for ten yards. He settled down behind a rotting stump, checked his Ingram and waited.

A few minutes later a Japanese man with a flattop came around the bend in the trail. He paused and looked behind, then put his M-16 between his knees so he could use both hands to retie a band around his head.

Bolan fired a burst beside him.

"Don't move if you want to take another breath!" Bolan barked.

The man shivered, and the M-16 fell to the ground.

"Leave it there. Hands laced on top of your head—now!"

The man obeyed.

Bolan walked up with the Ingram aimed at the center of the weekend soldier's chest.

"Who are you and why are you trying to kill us?"

"My name is Tommy Yashita. I was obeying orders."

"What orders?"

"To let no one pass through this area."

"Who gave the orders?"

"Sam Yamaguchi."

"He works for Dr. Dunning?"

"Dunning thinks so."

"How many gunmen like you does Yamaguchi have?"

"I'm not sure. Maybe twenty. Hell, a machine gun! He didn't tell us we'd be facing any of those."

"What is Yamaguchi planning?"

"Hell, you'll have to ask him."

"I will, if he's still alive. Right now, smartass, you're going to show us how to get up the mountain to the trailer. And no arguments or I pull the trigger."

"Okay, I'm out of the battle. I could have used the damn money, too."

"Move it—back to your two buddies. Maybe you can bury them."

It was ten minutes later when they came to the scene where the two bodies lay. Kitty was not there. He called softly, telling her it was safe.

She came from a perfectly concealed position and nodded at him, the MP-40 up and trigger-ready.

"Sorry," she said when she came in. "I should have known there would be more than one. You have saved my life."

"We're even. The important point is we're both alive and we have a willing guide. He's going to take us right up the mountain to the trailer."

"Uh-huh, unless the lady wants to take out a half hour in the brush with them tight pants down."

Kitty smiled grimly at him and looked away. Suddenly she swung the submachine gun in a short arc, slamming the weapon against his chin. The man fell to the ground.

"Now, what were you saying?" Kitty asked him.

The flattop shook his head, holding his jaw. Blood was streaming from between his lips.

Bolan had examined the two bodies. There was nothing on either one that would identify them or help his search. He nudged their guide with his toe.

"Up, flattop—we've got to move."

Kitty took out a small transistor radio and listened to it for a moment. When she turned it off she gave Bolan a quick rundown on the news reports about the captured MIRV and the two explosions and Dr. Dunning's explanation why he did it.

"At least we know why he captured our MIRV," she said. "He is peace crazy. We have some of them on our side, too. He is crazy and thinks this will help. We had a nice balance of power before, a status of equality. Now he could be ruining it."

"And he might drop the next warhead on Russia or on the U.S. as another warning," Bolan said. "We better move up there and stop him."

Their guide walked with reluctance. Bolan stopped, grabbed his right arm and twisted it behind his back.

"In two seconds I can break your arm. And I won't hesitate if I think that will help you do what I say. Am I getting through to you?"

"Hey, I hear you. I'll show you the valley. It's right up the main road where it forks. No worry. I just want to come out of this thing alive. It's got me thinking a little."

"Probably too late. Let's move."

They jogged up the forestry road for a quarter of a mile to the fork. The heavy truck tire tracks led up the roadway to the left. Their flattop guide paced another hundred yards with them on the left arm of the trail and stopped.

"Look, man. My deal was I could stay alive. Now up there another hundred yards are a few man traps. A Nam thing to catch you. I'm not sure what it is. I can't go up there, because there's some kind of a blocking position with two men in it. They see me helping you and I get blown away. This is as far as I go. It's right on up there at the end of this little valley. Hell, I'd get off the road, go around their traps.''

Bolan's experience dealing with hostages and frightened persons told him the Japanese flattop was telling the truth. He was scared.

"Do you want to change your story? If you're lying to us, I'll come back here and cut your fingers off one at a time and make you eat them.''

The guide turned pale. "Look, man, I seen you blast my two buddies to hell. The blonde smashes me in the mouth with her machine gun. Don't you think I'm scared enough not to lie?''

"I hope so.'' Bolan used his last two riot cuffs and left the trussed up ex-guide in the brush beside the road. He bound the man's hands in front of him. In a couple of hours he could chew his way to freedom.

"Stay here. When we wipe out the problem up top, we'll come back for you. If you've lied to me, I'll be back quicker.''

Bolan motioned to Kitty to stay behind him as they began to move along the path. He used his K-Bar knife to cut a sturdy six-foot-long walking stick from a tree branch. Then they left the trail, heading into the trees. Bolan walked cautiously, testing every few steps with the stick, making sure the ground was solid. He had seen too many punji stake traps in Nam to blunder into one here.

The trip wire caught him by surprise. It was waist high between two trees, and made of a fine copper wire that he could not see. It broke at first contact. He only had time to grab Kitty as he dived to the ground, dragging her with him.

The explosion that rocked the pine forest was not a

concussion grenade. To Bolan it sounded like three fraggers tied together, triggering each other and scattering the deadly shrapnel over a large area.

Instinctively Bolan had ground his face into the pine mulch and crossed his arms over his head. When the sound of the zinging hot metal and the roar of the explosions died away, he heard Kitty gasping beside him.

"Damn!" she said, sucking in a breath. He sat up and saw blood on her blouse. Bolan unbuttoned it and peeled the cloth back as she watched. Her bra was bloody and he saw the shoulder strap had been cut by the shrapnel that had slashed across her upper chest over her left breast. The wound was two inches long, but the metal had not bitten deeply before it had exited.

She looked down at the blood. "Only a scratch. Let me get rid of the bra—it is ruined." She slipped out of her blouse, took off the bloody bra and looked up at him. "Now it is your turn to see me without clothes," she said with a little laugh that he noted with surprise was slightly nervous. She let him look at her full, rose-nippled breasts, then shrugged and put on her blouse.

Bolan pulled a package from his web belt, broke out a packet of dry medication and sprinkled it on the slash, then pressed on a giant-sized sticky bandage from the same envelope.

"That should stop the bleeding," he said. She cleaned the blood off her breast and side and buttoned her blouse.

"The man back there warned us about surprises, did he not," she said.

Bolan nodded.

The afternoon thunderstorm came suddenly, with jagged lightning cracking into the timber, and a light sprinkle showering them but only settling the dust, then it was over and the sun came out again.

They had kept moving slowly forward during the rain. Bolan wanted to move farther into the woods, but now in the filtered sunshine he could see more thin strands of copper wire gleaming between many of the trees. There were none straight ahead.

They moved forward slowly another ten yards, and Bolan probed with his walking stick at a bent sapling in the path. At once he jumped back. Something on the floor snapped, whipping the walking stick out of Bolan's hand. A thin nylon line jerked the stick twenty feet into the air, where it hung from the top of a small ponderosa tree that had been forced downward.

"A snare," Bolan said. "That could be you or me hanging upside down in that tree."

He cut another walking staff and they moved ahead. Bolan saw a dozen blinking strands of copper wire in the path. He cautioned her to get behind a tree, and he threw his walking stick ahead of him, then jumped behind a pine. Three grenades went off one after another as the stick triggered the trip wires. The shrapnel whizzed around, the sounds echoing into the trees.

"With this kind of a defense they sure don't want anyone discovering their transmission site up on top, or maybe the antenna," Bolan said.

They moved again, walking along a faint trail another twenty yards when Bolan suddenly started sinking into the ground. He lunged back just in time and caught Kitty's hand. She fell away from him, dragging him back to solid footing.

They sat on the ground, both panting from the sudden exertion, the surprise.

"A tiger pit," Kitty said. They pushed aside the camouflage and saw a six-foot-deep pit, four feet wide and six long, across the trail. On the bottom were two dozen sharpened stakes two inches thick, all pointing upward.

"Punji stakes," Bolan said. "It's one hell of a painful way to die." He tested the ground on each end of the trap and found another pit on the "safe" route around the end. The other end was solid ground.

"Try the radio," Bolan said. "Maybe there's more news."

The little set came on at once and was still tuned to the all-news station in Phoenix.

"There was absolutely no excuse for the Soviet Union to have warhead-loaded missiles orbiting the earth. The President launched what one official called an all-out campaign to discredit the Soviets for maintaining guided missiles in orbit after agreeing repeatedly over the last dozen years that such an act would grossly endanger the population of the entire world.

"The White House statement said the President had been in discussion with the Premier on the hot line about the problem, and that it had been decided to launch an immediate complaint with the United Nations and demand a Security Council session on this extremely dangerous and outrageous passive aggression by the Soviets.

"Reaction from other world capitals is also severe. London has branded the Russians warmongers, indicating that the missiles discovered in space are not defensive but purely offensive types, and as such can be considered only as a direct confrontation and aggression on the British nation. They say both economic and social sanctions will be considered against the Soviet Union at the first opportunity.

"Bonn, Rome, the Vatican, Paris, Stockholm, Mexico City, The Hague and Madrid also have sent messages described by all as 'stern, severe, outraged and serious' to the Soviets. Reaction is still pouring in, and the Soviets have so far said nothing in their own defense. The capture of the orbiter by a former brilliant NASA scientist, Dr. Peter Dunning, was a shock and complete surprise to the U.S. officials as well as the Soviets.

"Dunning has a history of attempting to downgrade U.S. reliance on offensive missiles and the use of antimissiles for defense instead. He resigned from NASA nearly two years ago, evidently to perfect his own capture system to show the world what the Soviets were actually doing in space."

The broadcast ended with sports news, and Kitty snapped off the radio. She shook her head. "I still do not believe they are Russian missiles. They could be American rockets just as well, and this special agent Dunning is only claiming they are Russian to make us look bad."

"But we don't have any orbiting MIRVs in space," Bolan said.

She nodded. "Of course you do. It has been a poorly kept secret. You cannot hide anything in space. That is how your Dr. Dunning knew something different was up there. We both have MIRVs in space. Yes, Dunning must have used two of the U.S. missiles, oh, probably without permission, but he is doing it all just to make us Russians look bad. My government has made no statement yet, yes? They have not denied the MIRV is theirs until they know exactly what missiles they have or do not have, and how the U.S. captured the missiles and what the purpose of this whole propaganda smear campaign really is. We are cautious."

Bolan laughed. "But why would Dunning capture one of his own country's missiles?"

"Strategy. Some devious scheme to make the Soviet Union look bad. You Americans do it all the time. Constant harassment about Jews emigrating from Russia, about our criminal writers whom you want to let loose on the world to spread their lies, about some of our mentally insane you say are political prisoners. Ridiculous. You never let up on us."

"Kitty. A free press and a free people such as we have in the United States are not directed by government what to say or think. We are free to do as we please. When we see injustice, here at home or overseas, we speak up. When we see a whole people held under a totalitarian police state system, we have an honest concern for the welfare of those millions of people."

"We will speak no more politics," she sniffed. "We will find Dr. Dunning and get the truth from him." She took the lead up the slope.

A second later the sound of small-arms and machine-gun fire erupted behind them. Bolan dropped to the ground and looked where they had just passed. They had moved apart instinctively. Disperse, don't let one lucky round kill a whole group. It was basic infantry training. He listened. More firing. An occasional sound of a grenade, but he could see no explosive smoke or hear any bullets whipping through the trees.

A moment later he heard more firing close by. But again no whining lead. He was about to stand, thinking it was a pair of remote-controlled and timed loud-speakers when an M-16 opened up twenty yards just ahead of them. Humming 5.56mm slugs chewed a path through pine needles over Bolan's head.

He crawled forward to the side of a log and saw that

Kitty had found cover behind a tree. A grenade sailed toward them and Bolan judged the distance. It would hit, roll and stay on the far side of the log. It did, exploding with a jarring blast that left his ears rattling.

Bolan edged up to look over the fallen trunk, but saw no enemy. He crawled to the end of the log fifteen feet away and stood up behind a large tree. This time when he looked around, he saw someone move in the brush. The Executioner watched again and brought up the Ingram. Branches parted and a curious face peered out.

Japanese.

Bolan sent a volley of parabellum rounds into the brush, hosing it down with a figure eight.

He heard Kitty fire her chatter gun just after he did, apparently at a different target. There was no more movement in the brush. To the left Bolan heard a scream of pain. He looked and saw Kitty standing behind a tree.

She motioned for him to cover her as she moved forward, and before he could tell her not to, she slid around the pine and ran.

He turned the Ingram and sent spaced single shots into the general area in front of Kitty until his magazine ran dry. He jammed in a new one and fired 3-round bursts into the potential enemy positions.

Her weapon chattered again, then all was silent. A few minutes later she appeared where he had fired at the Oriental face and waved him forward.

He thought she was crazy to take chances like that. He ran up and found another dead flattop.

"One more over there," she said. "Looks like they have been dug in here for some time. Candy wrappers, cigarettes, even portable two-way radios. Now somebody knows we are here and moving up the hill."

Bolan picked up one of the small radios and listened, but there was no transmission.

"That other firing we heard. . ." Kitty began.

"Probably loudspeakers, but we don't have time to find out."

They moved forward again, off the trail, through the brush, working their way toward the top of the small valley. The land slanted up, and now there was no semblance of a trail.

Bolan noted there was no more thin copper wire. He had never known how many were fake and how many real, but the threat had kept him channeled in one direction.

They broke through a fringe of brush and ponderosa and found themselves at the top of the valley on a small ridge. Beyond it was another timbered ridge and then a higher one and behind that still a higher one. To their right they could see the rise of the tallest point around, which Bolan had seen marked Horse Knoll on the map.

"We've been had," Bolan said, lowering the Ingram. "We've been conned into taking the route they wanted us to. This was a damn false lead to burn up time. Now we've got to get back down to that other fork in the road. That had to be the real one and this the sucker lead. We better get moving."

"The mighty American agent goofed," Kitty said.

They both moved across the finger ridge and worked down the other side, hoping to run into the forestry road. They could save half a mile of brush crashing. Time was running out. He dared not think what Dr. Dunning would do with the remaining twenty-two warheads of which he now had total control.

12

Bolan and Kitty worked downslope through the trees and the light brush for half an hour, but did not come to the road. Suddenly it was dusk, with full darkness only minutes away.

"There's no sense in continuing. We won't find the road in the dark," Bolan said. "We should get some sleep and move out very early in the morning."

"Good, I could get lost in here. Every tree looks just like the last one."

Bolan located a thick stand of scrub cedar and crashed through until he found a clearing. He scooped moss from some downed logs and placed it over pine boughs for a bed.

Kitty approached him and put her hand on his shoulder.

"Mack, there is one thing we should get taken care of so it won't hurt our operation."

"What's that?"

"This male-female thing. Sex. It bothers me—does it not affect you?"

"Of course—you're a beautiful lady."

"So why do we not take care of it right now?" She reached out and kissed his lips. Her arms came around him tightly. Then she led him to the moss-and-pine-bough bed and sat down. Kitty unbuttoned her blouse and reached up for him.

"Mack, we are not enemies now, not on the opposite sides. We are working together. We can forget personal angers."

Bolan knew she was partly right. They both had to live for the moment because the next one might never come. He sat beside her, leaned over and kissed her soft mouth and they lay down gently. She slipped off her blouse and they were in each other's arms, each meeting the needs of the other.

Darkness closed around them but they hardly noticed as they made love softly and eagerly, leaving their politics behind, forgetting their own private hells and trying only to satisfy the desires of the other.

Much later, fatigue overtook them and lulled by the forest stillness, they mellowed into sleep.

AT THE SAME TIME on the high slope of Horse Knoll, Dr. Peter Dunning was hard at work.

"Watch that cycle, Sam! Tell me when we're on cycle again and in perfect electrical production."

Dunning fiddled with his control board, made certain of his tracking procedures and that he was on target. Emotion surged through him and he smiled.

The second shoe was about to drop on the world. The second surprise for everyone, and especially for NASA. He had been amused by the scathing comments the U.S. had made about the Russian MIRVs. That really took guts! Maybe they did not remember what he knew. He shunted it all aside when Sam called out that he had cycle.

Dr. Dunning tracked the orbiter again to be sure, then punched into the computer instructions to send the five thousand commands rocketing through space toward the hardware high overhead. The commands were all variables of the code words needed to gain access to the computer on board the orbiter. On this one he was more familiar with the codes, and so created fewer with the aid of the computer.

He triggered the transmission, sat back and waited. In less than a minute the screen in front of him lighted up with a visual response. He had contact. Now to capture and then change the code words. He was the proud new owner of a second missile. But this one was the property of NASA and the United States of America!

He punched out messages and commands, gave an illogical command-access code to the on-board computer, making it impossible for NASA to retain control of the space vehicle. He ordered it to respond only to his commands. He did not interfere with the orbit or the regular informational transmissions of the MIRV.

Then he sat back and grinned. He laced his fingers together behind his head and told Sam about the capture. The man merely nodded. He was a cold one.

They kept the power up. Another public broadcast for him was coming soon. He checked his watch. Slightly after 8:00 P.M. Mountain time. That would make it 10:00 P.M. in Washington, D.C.

He adjusted his dials and controls, and beamed his signal at the World Wide Communications satellite in geosynchronous parking orbit 22,000 miles over Chicago. He overrode certain controls and sent directions to the satellite, which broke in on regular programs and broadcast on all three TV networks his audio. With his modemlike device he could surge-transmit, send ten minutes of dialogue to the satellite in eight to ten seconds. The satellite would then rebroadcast it. Such a surge made it almost impossible to catch and trace the source of the transmission.

His talk had been recorded and computer-processed, and now when he was sure he had the right combination of signals, he pressed the Send button, and his words shot through space to the communications satellite.

Three minutes later, at 7:14 P.M. Pacific time and 10:14 Eastern time, the three networks turned into an audio forum for Dr. Dunning. The sound came over strongly, but the picture remained the same. The one hundred million Americans listening to TV at that moment heard Dr. Dunning make history.

"My fellow Americans, I want to take this opportunity to tell you of a new development in the world of space. As you know, yesterday I captured a Russian MIRV orbiter Armageddon, filled with twenty-four death-dealing hydrogen warheads. Tonight I have just captured another missile. However this one is owned by and was put into orbit secretly by the United States. It grieves me to have to tell you this. It hurts me that our government would do something like this, an act they called 'infamous' and 'beastly' when the Russians' orbiters were made known.

"Our officials at NASA and the White House will tell you we were 'forced' to put up the MIRVs because we knew the Russians had them in place. It is impossible to hide anything in orbit. It's up there for anyone's radar to detect and evaluate. For almost three years now we and the Russians have had the MIRVs orbiting over our living rooms. This was with the full knowledge and approval of our Congress. It is time to stop this dangerous situation and to get the missiles down.

"The solution is simple. I am holding the world hostage with my remaining hydrogen-bomb-tipped missiles. I will continue to hold you hostage until the Soviet Union and the United States destroy all the remaining

MIRVs in orbit around the earth or disassemble them. Yes, the U.S. also had twelve of these vehicles in orbit.

"The U.S. and Russia may work out between them how this is to be done, but the best solution is to have one complete MIRV on each side fired into a sun orbit. Then when radar shows that one MIRV has been fired from each side, the second two are fired, and so on until all are in sun orbit where they will eventually fall into the sun and explode with no damage to the universe.

"Expensive? Misguided defensive-offensive weapons always are expensive. And both sides will lose, but on the other hand the world will gain a more stable peace, and the dangers of an accidental hydrogen holocaust will be greatly reduced. I am giving the great powers twelve hours to accept my terms. If they do not, both the U.S. and Russia will suffer a terrible, unspeakable tragedy.

"Now, the threat. I hold the big stick. I could wipe out both Moscow and Washington if I chose. Instead, I have a similar threat to hand to the rulers of both nations. If the agreement is not made within twelve hours to begin simultaneous destruction of all MIRVs now in orbit, and agreement is not made to put no more in space, one city in America and one city in Russia of ten thousand persons will be targeted by a single hydrogen warhead from its own nation and obliterated from the face of the earth.

"Then, when the horror of the twenty thousand deaths hits the consciences of the world, there will be a total uproar and the big powers will be forced by economic boycotts, social and political action and moral suasion to destroy the horrendous weapons both now illegally have in orbit.

"Mr. President, you should contact me through the normal radio network. I will be listening for your reply.

"The decision is in your hands. Destroy your MIRVs or sacrifice twenty thousand lives, and then wait for my next ultimatum, which will be more terrible, more destructive and will cost many, many more lives."

The broadcast continued for the ten minutes as Dunning gave his reasons for demanding that the world begin to pull back from the use and the threat of use of such devastating weapons. He showed how defensive measures were more practical, less costly and more effective. When the talk ended it was repeated three more times, blocking out all commercial network TV for forty minutes.

The whole world was immediately alerted. An emergency meeting of the President and his top advisors was called within five minutes after the ultimatum was given. NASA refused public comment. A press conference was promised by the President within "a few hours." Speculation ran wild all over the radio and TV talk shows and newscasts.

ON THE MOUNTAIN in Arizona, Bolan awoke. Something stirred him. Kitty lay beside him, still asleep. He reached for the small radio they had listened to and turned it on. The all-news station came in softly but clear. It was 2:30 A.M.

There was only one story on the air that night. The station alternated playing a tape of the TV audio by Dr. Dunning and getting various experts from around the country to comment on the threat. Bolan turned the set off and thought it through.

Dunning had the world by the balls. There was no alternative. The great powers would feel so pressured by world opinion that they would bow to his demands. He would win his war without firing a shot!

For a moment Bolan thought of abandoning his search for Dr. Dunning. If he could have his twelve hours, Dr. Dunning very well could rid the world of this orbiting disaster. He had no selfish motive. He was dealing strictly from a superior ethical-moral-antiwar basis. Bolan thought of slipping away from the Russian and moving up the mountain alone. He doubted she would share his views about the correctness of what Dr. Dunning was trying to do. She would hear about the ultimatum as soon as she woke up and turned on the radio.

Bolan made up his mind what to do, then lay down on the moss-and-pine mattress and drifted quickly to sleep.

The Executioner awoke again at five-thirty. A few faint streaks of light penetrated the forest. Kitty sat up at once, buttoned her blouse and pulled on her jeans and boots. Then she turned on the radio. There was still only one big news story.

"Listen to this!" she said.

When she understood the substance of the story, she stood and shouldered her weapon.

"Come on, we must hurry. We need to get up there just as fast as we can now to stop this terrorist. He has the whole world as hostage and he keeps making those crazy demands." She stopped and turned. "Or maybe you don't think they are so strange."

"Did you know about the MIRVs in orbit?" he asked.

"I suspected. I knew we had the technology and hardware to do it, and I thought it was a great strategy, only not to be kept a secret. What power!"

"I didn't know any of them were up there. I figured it was possible, but not that it was done. This had to be the best kept U.S. secret since the atomic bomb work."

"But you did not answer my question. You don't seem outraged about Dr. Dunning's plans."

"Frankly, I think it's a good idea. I don't like fighting science. Give me a man in a foxhole and we both have the same chance. These missiles swinging down on me from orbit with zero early warning...I'm just old-fashioned enough not to like it. If I could choose, I would go along with Dr. Dunning."

She bristled and turned the radio up louder.

"We now have special reports from Rome and London. As happened over Moscow and Washington, D.C., hydrogen warheads exploded high over both Rome and London last night. There was no damage. The explosions again lighted up the night sky like day, and were seen as another warning from Dr. Dunning that he could obliterate any city he wanted anywhere on earth. There was no response from Dr. Dunning after the spectacular display of what experts said were the explosions twenty-five thousand miles in space. Events have moved swiftly since the Russians first charged the Americans with 'spacenapping' one of their satellites.

"Now the world faces an uncertain future. On one hand is the threat of twenty thousand deaths if the big powers do not begin to destroy the outer-space bombs. On the other hand, if Dr. Dunning fails, there is the constant threat of hydrogen missiles falling on cities at any time of the day or night, whether by design or some unforeseen earth-shattering accident. The opinion we have sampled around the world is that the only option the Russian and American governments have is to comply with Dr. Dunning's demands."

Kitty snapped off the radio. In her hand was the Luger aimed at Mack Bolan's chest.

"Now, Mack, we march up that mountain and relieve Dr. Dunning of his little space station. Move!"

13

In the White House the President looked out an Oval Office window. He had heard the broadcast about the missing U.S. MIRV at 10:22 P.M. By stages he had been outraged, furious, embarrassed at the world image the U.S. had lost, angry, in awe of Dr. Dunning and then furious again.

"He can't do that to us!" the President had raged once around midnight.

His NASA chief calmly pointed out that Dunning already had raped them, and now he was looking for the plaudits.

"He caught us horsewhipping the Russians for having MIRVs up there, and then slapped us in the face by showing the world that we were doing the very same thing."

Anyone with any clout was there. Most had given opinions, made pitches and sat back. The secretary of state summed it up.

"Mr. President, I don't see anything else we can do but what he asks. He has us in a no-win situation. We had our chance when he knocked down that communications satellite. We should have nailed the son of a bitch right there. Now, we pay for it. There is no way we can let him drop a hydrogen bomb on one of our towns and kill ten thousand people. Absolutely no way. And there is not a chance that we can blow up our MIRVs unless the Russians do the same."

The President scowled. "Gentlemen, the Premier told me during our last talk a half hour ago that if their sensors find one incoming missile, they will launch a massive first strike against our mainland. When we sense their incoming, we will be forced to launch our retaliation strike, and suddenly we are in the middle of an everyone-lose thermonuclear war."

"A bluff. The Premier is bluffing, Mr. President," Secretary of Defense Jensen said. "Hell, he knows he'd get clobbered if he tried that. No way he's going to start a third world war. No chance at all. It's a bluff."

"We still have no direct communication with Dr. Dunning?" the President asked.

"None, Mr. President," the NASA man said. "Only the network radio where he listens. Then he talks to us by taking over some network broadcast."

Everyone was quiet for a moment.

"Mr. President, a compromise," Ron Harloff said. He was the Russian interpreter and the vice-president looked at him furiously. He was not supposed to offer suggestions. The President waved the VP off and motioned for Harloff to go ahead.

"I've been listening to the tone, the inflections the Premier uses. He's looking for a face-saving measure. We compromise not with him but with Dr. Dunning. Suppose we say we have technical problems with massive sunspots or a new set of quasars or some such, and while we can't dump all of the MIRVs right now we will move one out fifty thousand miles into space and explode it, the way he asked. We ask him for two weeks to work out the diplomatic problems with the other ten MIRVs on each side.

"That way we lost one more MIRV, but we hold off on the deaths and we placate Dr. Dunning for two weeks. He knows how slow it is to negotiate with the Russians. In that two weeks we have plenty of time to move our tracking people in and find his location. We can get the Premier to go along with this by saying within that two weeks we can find and neutralize Dr. Dunning and give the Russians back control of the captured vehicle."

The President nodded. "Might work. Just might work. Only instead of dumping that first MIRV, why not say we need another twenty-four hours before we can do that—the testing, the systems checks, everything that is set up on a new twenty-four-hour countdown. We can tell the Premier that we should be able to nail Dr. Dunning within twenty-four hours. Now, how close are we to finding him?"

Gregory, the NASA chief, shook his head. "Not close. We swept the area with our radio scanners, and no luck. He was in Arizona, so he might still be there. But there are a ton of mountains there to comb through."

"But the Premier doesn't know that," the President said. "Yes, I think we can buy another twenty-four hours. What time is it?"

"Six-thirty."

"Good. Set up a quick talk with the Premier. And if any of you have any other ideas how we can convince the Premier we're about ready to catch Dunning, let's have them now."

"What do we have to start the hunt?" Jensen asked.

"We have one transmission fix of about twenty seconds," Gregory said. "But it's a one-liner going from Houston straight across the western half of the country."

"I'd like to see the route," Jensen said. "It's a damn

sight better than sitting here on our asses doing nothing.'' The two men left and moved down the hall to a special war room.

Ron Harloff made the hot-line connection to Russia and spoke briefly with his counterpart in Moscow. Twenty seconds later the leaders of the world's two largest countries were talking.

''Mr. Premier, good day. Yes, yes, the weather is hot here, too. Moscow in summer—I've heard about it. Now, Mr. Premier, I have an idea I wanted to check with you. First, let me say I don't like to knuckle under to blackmail. However, in this case it is going to be most difficult not to. But we have a chance.''

After the translation, the Premier spoke rapidly.

''Mr. President, this sounds like Western talk. We still think it is some kind of a NASA plot, but we don't know what. Yes, we know one of your missiles has been moved slightly and he says captured, but NASA could have done that.''

''Mr. Premier, believe me, I wish it were so. Then I wouldn't have been up for thirty-six hours trying to figure this out. Our plan is to buy twenty-four more hours from Dr. Dunning. We agree to explode the first MIRV in far space. But we have a twenty-four-hour safety countdown system that must be worked through before any MIRV can be activated. A safety system. I think he'll accept that. This should give us time for our FBI and our communications people to find Dr. Dunning and capture him. That's our plan I want to try to sell to Dunning.''

''I do not like it!'' the Premier shouted. ''It is a trick. I do not even like the idea that we think of giving in to this blackmailer, this extortionist, this reactionary.''

''Fine, Mr. Premier. Then we sit here and watch

twenty thousand innocent men, women and children, American and Russian, vaporized. You say that will start World War Three. Strike and counterstrike and you and I will bring death and destruction to forty percent of the world's population. It means that civilization as we know it will not survive. We all will be back in caves within two days eating rats.''

''No, not that either.''

''Then do you have a better plan?''

The President and Harloff could hear the Premier of Russia heave an exasperated sigh.

''No. With much reluctance I agree to your plan. Capture this madman and make him suffer. Your secret police must work fast. We hope that you can capture him in the twenty-four hours.''

''We will do our best, Mr. Premier.''

Ron Harloff translated the goodbyes, and put the two phones away in locked drawers.

Secretary of Defense Jensen came back into the office and caught the President's weary glance.

''Sir. If I could show you something?''

The President nodded. Jensen spread out on a desk a map of the southwestern United States.

''We have a bearing on that one transmission from our Houston listening post. This is a line drawn across the western section of the country. There are six or seven areas where Dunning could be holed up. We think he would want to get high enough to eliminate trash electrical signals that would interfere, since he wouldn't have the equipment needed to filter them all out.

''This could put him in the San Mateo Mountains in New Mexico or the Managas Mountains on the Continental Divide, also in New Mexico. In Arizona it might be some of the Mogolion Mountains in the Rim area.

Over in California we have the line going across the Shadow Mountains and Bald Mountains in the Sierra Nevada. Any of these areas are potential transmission spots. We're ordering air units out as soon as it's daylight in those regions, with radar, triangulation equipment and special heat-sensor scopes to check out any unusual situations. We could have reports back in as little as three hours.''

"Good. It's a chance, a long one, but a chance. Take along some of that new space-photo equipment and get pictures of anything that looks unusual.''

"Yes, sir. We're moving on that right now.''

The President talked to his press secretary, shaking his head. "So we've got the Premier's go-ahead, and now all we have to do is write something that will convince Dr. Dunning. Get somebody right on it. I'll read the message on the air myself. This has to be damn convincing. Because Dunning has been shooting off rockets from up there. We've got to make him believe this is a new procedure he doesn't know about. Make it good. Get back to me in an hour.'' The President seemed to slump a little. "Maybe Jensen's planes can find something with his peekaboo cameras out there. Hell, I hope so.''

The press secretary hurried off to another room where four speech writers had been standing by to offer assistance.

The President brightened as an aide spoke to him.

"Gentlemen, a little good news. If you're willing to take shifts of eight at a time, we can have some breakfast in the south dining room. Anyone hungry?''

14

Mack Bolan was not surprised by the KGB agent's reaction to his praise for Dr. Dunning and his purpose in this hijack. He had thought it through and figured she would react this way. He looked at the Luger and smiled.

"You actually think you can force me to help you do something I really do not want to do?"

"I have the gun, remember?"

"Yeah, right. And I refuse to help you, then you shoot me, and in five minutes flat you're so lost you can't even find the car again, much less get to the top of the right mountain where Dr. Dunning is. You couldn't figure your way out of a clover patch in broad daylight in Central Park."

He watched her, saw the indecision building.

"Sure, hell, yes," Bolan continued, "I'm bluffing—think what you like. But are you sure you can find the way back to the car? Where is that valley we just blundered our way through? Which direction?"

He saw she was frowning as she stared up at the trees around them, then at the slope. Slowly she lowered the Luger.

"You cannot be sure Dunning will do what he says. It could all be a trick of some kind, some way to get our MIRVs destroyed and leave your MIRVs in space. That would be a tremendous tactical and psychological advantage."

"Hey, that would be nice. But you're forgetting neither NASA nor the President knows anything about this super strategy you've worked out for them. It's Dunning acting on his own, and as you say, nobody can be sure of what he's going to do. So, dammit, maybe we should keep on moving and go up to the top of the mountain, wherever it is, and have a little chat with him."

The woman hesitated. She glanced up quickly. "Are you not going to ask me for my gun?"

"No. Why should I? We're partners—a team, remember?"

"You are laughing at me."

"We don't have time to laugh; we have to find our way up this beast of a mountain."

It took Bolan an hour to sort out the hills and valleys and get back on the main forestry trail that would lead them upward toward Horse Knoll. Again he could see the tracks of the heavy vehicle. In soft spots the tires sank six inches into the ground. They met no more opposition for two miles. Bolan was thankful that it was not an in-depth defense, with each circle of protectors becoming deeper, more heavily armed and more proficient. He hoped Yamaguchi had concentrated most of his troops at the access roads, planning to chop off any inquisitive or lightly armed forces there.

They came around a curve in the roadway and Bolan saw a tree across the trail. It was a good-sized piñon. They ran into the thinner cover at the side of the trail.

"Trouble," Bolan said.

"We go together," Kitty said. "I will not give you the chance to lose me out here." She lifted the submachine gun. "You know I can use this, right? We stay close together and support each other."

"Side by side," Bolan said and moved through the pine and light brush toward the roadblock ahead.

The woman was starting to present a problem. He was not sure what he would do when he got to the top. Yamaguchi still bothered Bolan. Why would Dr. Dunning give "kill" orders now after being so careful and spending so much time, effort and money to be sure that he killed no one back at the mesa? It didn't make sense. Unless.... He thought it through again. That could be an answer.

Unless Yamaguchi was not following orders, unless Yamaguchi had thoughts of taking over for himself. What was it the captured soldier had said? Yamaguchi had this little group...mostly National Guardsmen...maybe thirty men. A chill sweat popped out on Bolan's forehead. Suddenly he felt like ditching his companion and racing up the hill to find out for sure what was going on there. But he must wait.

They moved carefully from tree to tree. At first there seemed to be no one around the roadblock. Maybe it was a windfall. Bolan was twenty yards to one side when Kitty broke into the open and sent a 5-round group of lead messengers into the limbs of the horizontal pine.

"Hey, take it easy. I sure as hell ain't no goddamned whitetail deer," a voice shouted. A man emerged from behind the log, his hands at his sides. Kitty looked at him and shook her head. Bolan had the right angle. Another figure stood up behind a tree out of Kitty's sight line and lifted an M-16 to his shoulder. Bolan's Ingram rattled ten rounds in a tight circle. They caught the gunman across his chest and then again through his groin. He jolted backward out of sight behind the fallen conifer.

Kitty swung her weapon that way and in a blink the

first flattopped defender brought up a handgun and fired at Kitty. She swept the submachine gun back, already firing and cutting the young Japanese man in two before he could shoot again.

Kitty and Bolan dropped to the ground as the echoes of the gunfire faded slowly into the hills.

After five minutes of movement, no sound, Bolan stood.

"That should do it." There were only two of them. Whoever was up on top knew they were coming now for sure.

Kitty came slowly through the trees. At first she would not look at him.

"Don't worry about it—you're still alive. Now we should make some time. I've got a hunch that was the last bit of defense between here and the end of the rainbow up there. Any news on that radio of yours?"

"Do not patronize me. I made a bad mistake and could have got us both killed. Luckily it did not happen."

"Hell, half of this business is luck."

She turned on the small radio and held it so they could hear the news station.

"Dr. Peter Dunning, our resident mad scientist who now is camped out on some mountaintop, continued to hold the world powers at bay today. He refused a last-minute appeal by the President of the United States, speaking for himself and the Russian Premier, with a request for a twenty-four-hour delay in the deadline to send one of the MIRVs from each nation into deep space and destroy it.

"Since no additional time was granted, the United States has reported that it fired one of its twenty-four-warhead MIRVs into deep space and exploded all of them in one gigantic bang. Observatories around the world reported the detonation.

"So far Russia has not sent one of her missile clusters to be exploded. The deadline is past, and the President has warned Russia if a MIRV comes into its landmass it will be coming from one of their own missiles controlled by Dr. Dunning and not from any United States action.

"There has been no word from Dr. Dunning. World opinion is peaking, and it is against the Soviet Union. The President has said he now agrees with Dr. Dunning that there should be no orbiting weapons of any kind in space. He says he is ready either to bring those in space back, or at least to salvage their warheads to cut the massive dollar loss to the American taxpayers.

"Meanwhile, a community of action and reaction is building across the world to severely chastise both the U.S. and Russia for orbiting the deadly weapons. Some say that it is the biggest groundswell of public outcry since the Russians went into Afghanistan several years—"

The radio suddenly cut off and Bolan smiled, wondering how long she could listen to the criticism of her homeland.

"So far we haven't thrown out the bombs with the bathwater," Bolan said. Kitty looked at him with a puzzled expression. "An old country expression," he said, and she was more confused than ever.

They were making progress. The trail wound around the side of the mountain now, and ahead Bolan could see a bald area. They hiked for another half mile, and Bolan sat down in the shade next to a tree.

"Conference time," Bolan said. "We're getting close. From here on we move slowly, carefully, under cover and far off the road. It will be our guide only. We want to get up there and find out what kind of a defensive setup Yamaguchi has for us. He knows for sure that we're coming. I'm still not certain how he fits into this picture. He's changed the tone from benign to deadly.

"When we do find them, we don't go charging in. We regroup and I'll go out on recon and see what I can find out. Then we do what we need to. You keep that radio on so we know as much as we can what is going on in Moscow and Washington and in outer space. Any suggestions?"

"That was not a conference, it was a listing of instructions." She looked away. "Still, I can offer no better plan. But I want to get as close as we can before you go on your recon."

15

Dr. Peter Dunning sat at his console and smiled. He had done it! He had forced the destruction of twenty-four horrendous warheads! But there were still hundreds of them to go. The Russians would come around and kick their MIRV into outer space soon. He was sure of it. But just to goad them on a little, he would send them one more warning. He set up his console to bounce a radio signal off the satellite and override the three networks' normal transmissions. When he had a firm access, he began.

"This is a special message to the Russian Premier. I hope the translation will be accurate. Mr. Premier, you now have four hours to complete your assigned task of destroying one of your MIRV missile carriers and its twenty-four hydrogen bombs. It can be ejected into outer space or sent farther out and triggered for automatic destruction. The choice is yours. The United States has already complied and you are now nearing a danger period when one single warhead could be launched against that village of ten thousand persons inside Russia. Remember, you have only four hours more!"

Dunning sat back and laughed softly, then switched off the controls. Now he would wait. There was no reasonable way the Russians would not comply. He saw Sam Yamaguchi come in.

"Sam, it's going to be champagne and steak tonight, my friend! We're on the way. The hardest part, that first missile destruction, is over. Now we have clear sailing. I predict that the Russians will have their MIRV destroyed within two hours."

Yamaguchi shrugged. "It really doesn't matter one way or the other."

"Oh, you're wrong there, my friend. It matters a great deal. The whole future of the human race as we know it today just may hinge on what you and I are doing here."

"Then we may be in one hell of a jam," the Oriental said. He pulled a .45 automatic pistol from behind him and aimed it at his boss.

"Sam! I told you not to bring that up here. Now put it away at once. You know I don't like guns."

"Hey, that's just tough, doc, because from now on you're going to be seeing one hell of a lot of them. Come and look outside."

"What do you mean?" Dunning asked, puzzled.

"Come take a look out the trailer door."

They went to the door and Dr. Dunning stopped at once.

"My God, what have you done?"

"I'm taking over, doc, and if you want to argue, you can start by fighting off this bunch."

Outside the trailer were ten men. All wore combat-green camouflage uniforms. All had M-16 rifles and a few held submachine guns. All had packs and blanket rolls, combat webbing, and to Dr. Dunning they looked like hardened troops ready for battle.

"You're taking over? What in the world for? You're a good worker, but you have almost no concept of the mass destruction that would be produced by any global thermonuclear war. I'm totally taken aback."

Yamaguchi spun the .45, put it in a holster he now strapped on and caught a larger weapon one of his men on the ground tossed him. Dr. Dunning assumed it was one of those terrorist-type submachine guns.

"Damn right I'm not interested in any of that crap. What I am interested in is the raw *power* that you have just grabbed hold of and you don't even realize it. Let me spell it out for you in simple language. I have taken over this whole damn outfit. I have men at the roads to keep anyone from coming up here. I have a gun in your stomach and I control the access and the transportation. The only way you stay alive is to do exactly what I tell you. If I say send a message to all the TV stations via the satellite, you do it and quick. You will do precisely and exactly what I tell you to if you want to keep on living. Is that clear?"

"Sam, sometimes the quality of life is much more important than just staying alive."

"But you will do what I tell you!"

"Yes. I have to be here to protect all of this, and perhaps along the way somewhere you'll tell me what you're trying to accomplish."

"Hell, doc, didn't I tell you that? What I'm going to accomplish is get rich and make all of my friends rich."

"Blackmail? You're going to hijack the whole planet?" Dr. Dunning laughed. "Sam, you certainly do think big—I have to give you credit for that."

"You don't know just how big yet." Yamaguchi signaled to one of the men who left the group and ran up to Sam.

Dr. Dunning noticed that he, too, had a flattop haircut and was Japanese. They talked for a moment in what Dr. Dunning guessed was Japanese, then Sam turned.

"Dr. Dunning, this is my friend and computer and telecommunications expert, Harry. He will be your shadow. He is familiar with most of this equipment and what we will need. If he tells you to do something, you do it. We will be turning on the equipment now and making a transmission through the radio net via the satellite as usual. But this time I will be doing the talking."

"And if I refuse?"

"Then you die and we go ahead with our plans, anyway."

"It seems you have the upper hand right now."

"I always had—you just didn't know it."

Someone ran into the open space near the trailer and spoke with one of the soldiers. This one, too, wore a uniform. He was pointed to Sam, who watched as he came up.

The man bowed, but his expression showed fear.

"Bad news, Sam. Someone is coming. We lost two men at the second roadblock. I didn't see anyone but I heard their automatic fire. I went around another way, and when I got there both our men were dead."

"Not in English, you fool!"

"Dead? These men of yours are killing?" Dunning asked.

Yamaguchi caught the scientist by the shirt and pushed him back in the trailer.

"No, not killing—two of ours were killed. Two of mine are dead. So now it's more important than ever that we make that first broadcast. Set up right now to transmit on that radio frequency you use to the satellite. And do it quickly. We don't want them to triangulate and find our position—not yet, anyway."

HIGH OVER THE SOUTHWEST, Air Force planes had been combing the mountains along the line from Houston to San Francisco since daylight. They had found nothing. Twice the coded transmissions had gone out to the satellite, but on and off so quickly that the triangulation could not be accomplished. Now the aircraft crew needed some kind of extended transmission in order to lock onto it positively.

The crew reported some indicators—some fragmentary crossing lines—had been established, but ones still too vague to be reliable. The crosses seemed to be either in Arizona or western California. The troops were told to concentrate in that area.

High over the imaginary line a vintage U-2 spy plane refitted with the latest aerial photo equipment cruised along, shooting two hundred frames every ten seconds. The pilot was not sure what he was looking for. He had been rolled out of bed and pitched into the cockpit before he was fully awake. Now he slanted over the border of New Mexico and headed into Arizona.

IN WASHINGTON, D.C., they paced and waited. The immediate transmission and crossing reference lines had not materialized and now it looked as if it wouldn't be as easy to find as they had at first hoped.

Secretary of Defense Jensen kept ordering more and more aircraft into the sky. He had worked that line from Houston to San Francisco dozens of times. Sometimes the planes had been at nearly treetop level. So far nothing had turned up in the personal observations or in the quick-developing film. Time, it was going to take more time, and each hour longer it took meant the chance of losing another MIRV. The damn Russians better kick theirs out soon, Jensen thought, or there was going to be international hell to pay.

The President sat in the Oval Office. In the background a network radio station played softly. Now the people knew, the whole damn world knew, that there were killer missiles up there just waiting for somebody to push a button and send them down.

So fast! Thousands of years of civilization could be wiped out in half an hour of warfare. Nobody had the right! Yes, he had to be thinking that way. The American public would not stand for the MIRVs' being up there. Not now that they knew—if the Russians brought them down, too. It was a standoff. The Soviets had the missiles up first and we caught up to "balance" the potential danger.

Except then it had been a private standoff. Now everyone in the world knew. And the world would demand that both the U.S. and Russia bring down safely or destroy all such MIRVs and any other kind of weapon in space. It was going to be damn tricky, this one, damn tricky. And the President almost wished that his successor had it to deal with. No, hell, no! He would accept that responsibility himself.

Ten minutes earlier the Premier had agreed to explode their MIRV in outer space. It would be a test of the destruct system if nothing else. The President had not told the world yet, or the networks. He had to soon so the madman on the hill somewhere would know. It had been one hell of a tough day so far, and the President had a feeling that his troubles were only just beginning.

16

Mack Bolan bellied up to the side of the big ponderosa. He pushed higher so he could see past the root mass and found his ears had been right. Ahead in the heavier cover, he could see two men digging foxholes. Both wore camou green, were armed and digging fast. Bolan's combat mind quickly evaluated the situation. An outpost, a listening post. He checked the area behind them. The men were on a gentle slope, one on each side of the road.

It should not be much farther to the top of the mountain. Bolan knew the trailer would not be parked out in the middle of the bald area. It would be under some heavy cover.

The trail here was not steep but wound around the side of the mountain. The Executioner pulled back twenty yards and stayed out of sight as he worked his way silently around the two advance guards.

He had to get closer or he had to come to some kind of main line of resistance. He was not sure which. The two men back there had looked competent enough. Both had been Japanese, but he could not see their haircuts for the soft green caps.

When he was five hundred feet past the guards, Bolan worked back toward the road. It had leveled off and seemed to end a half mile ahead in a thick clump of tall pine and heavier brush. There were no troops that he

could see guarding the area. But they could be anywhere. Or they could be dug in along the roadway.

As he watched, a young man came jogging down the
road, his M-16 at port arms. And he looked as if he
knew what he was doing.

The runner vanished into the heavier timber and did
not show anywhere else. Bingo! Bolan jogged away
from the road, heading for the wooded part he figured
they would not expect trouble. A half hour later he was
slightly higher on the hill than his target.

He could see it spread out below—the camouflaged
trailer, the huge dish antenna pointing skyward, the
shape of the tractor covered with pine branches. Even
the dish skyreader had been painted in camouflage col-
ors. He doubted a pilot more than three hundred feet in
the air could see the setup.

Around the area he had spotted a dozen different
men. Once, a man in a white shirt came to the door of
the trailer and looked out, but he soon went back inside.
The defense of the position seemed to be in a crude circle, with twice the men on the area where the road came
in.

As the Executioner jogged back to the place where he
had left Kitty, he worked out his general strategy. He
would see just how good Kitty was with her chopper and
see how well the KGB field agent stood up against a few
mercenary flattops.

Kitty did not like the assignment.

"Again you are not conferring, you are directing."

"Fine, you go up there and see what you think. I'll
wait right here for you. Of course, don't get yourself
lost. A lot of green trees and brown hills between here
and there."

She stared hard at him for a minute. "You really are a

bastard, are you not?'' Then she grinned. ''Unfortunately you are the only bastard I have, so I will have to play along. You know we cannot waste the time for a double recon.''

''So shut up and listen,'' Bolan said in mock anger.

''We should get moving. We have enough daylight left?'' she asked.

''It won't be dark for six hours yet. You've got the signals straight?''

Kitty nodded. ''I do. I still do not know why you changed your mind and now you want to go in and stop them.''

''Yamaguchi. He must be in control. He has his own 'army.' He's given kill orders to his men. That isn't Dr. Dunning's style. He would never order any such actions. Which makes me wonder if Dunning is still in control up there.''

The afternoon thunderstorm was late, but when it came there was much thunder and lightning. The rain fell hard for fifteen minutes. It was a warm rain, but they were soaked even though they stood under a scrub cedar.

When it had passed they wiped off their weapons and moved out.

They went together the first mile. Then Kitty turned on the little radio and waved at him to listen.

''So that's all we know about it right now. From our reports from the network we understand it was the same type of 'takeover' that preceded each of the Dunning interferences with network broadcasting. This one had a different voice and a startlingly different message. We now have the tape and can play the message from what we assume to be the command post of this Dunning MIRV-hijacking center.'' There was a brief pause before the recorded broadcast began.

"Good morning, world. I just want to tell you I'm your new leader. The name isn't that important, so you can call me Mr. Richman, because that's what I'm going to be. You see, friends, I've done you all a great big favor. This is not Dr. Dunning speaking, as you have figured out by now.

"Not by a damn sight. I have taken control from Dr. Dunning. I have saved the world. Hell, I don't care if you guys have a hundred MIRVs up there. Not really. You can keep them all up there if you want to. I heard the Russkis finally fired off one of their MIRVs into space and blew it up. Fine. Who cares?

"Not me—I got other concerns. First, all you folks out there, and especially you governments, Mr. President and Mr. Premier of Russia, you guys owe me. I said owe me as in cash money. Here is what I want. . . no, what I demand! For saving the world, you must pay to me the sum of two hundred million dollars' worth of gem-quality uncut diamonds. I want them within twenty-four hours.

"Continue to communicate with me the same way you did with Dr. Dunning, through the radio networks. Do not attempt to find me or to locate this transmitter, or one of the MIRV missiles will be unleashed somewhere on the world. It will be targeted and aimed and fired, and I have just the man who can do it right here beside me.

"Remember, two hundred million in uncut diamonds. I'll be waiting for your reply within the next half hour. Goodbye my new friends. This is Mr. Richman signing off."

Kitty snapped off the radio.

"Now your American mad scientist had been captured by one of your crazy American hoodlums. You are an interesting people, I will admit that." She squinted as she looked at Bolan. "This little change in management does not mean a thing to me. He is probably more dangerous than the other one. What do you think?"

"We go in and get him. I had figured something like this. The two styles just didn't match up somehow. Not with all of Yamaguchi's firepower. We'd better hustle. Each of those guys in his army is a mercenary and looking for a big chunk of that two hundred million."

Ten minutes later they parted. Bolan checked the Childers combat shotgun he had tied to his back before they left the car. Now he was glad he had brought it. He circled the same way he had before, coming in from the "back door," where the reception would be less heated. He looked at his watch to be sure of his timing.

Kitty was supposed to take out the first guards she could find, as near to the trailer as possible. She might actually get a couple of them, but for sure it would send a surge of troops her way and give Bolan a quick shot at getting inside the defensive perimeter, with or without firing.

He was in position five minutes before attack time. He checked the scene and it was as before, but now Bolan saw a rocket launcher, and a small bipod-mounted machine gun. They were bringing out the heavy equipment. He had crawled to within twenty feet of the closest guard. The man had dug a hole of sorts and positioned himself behind a two-foot pine log and faced outward.

Bolan watched the second hand of his watch spin around for the last time, and when it hit 1515 hours he heard the stuttering of an automatic weapon across the compound from him. At least the KGB was on time. He watched the trooper in front of him and saw the man show himself, spin and yell something in a foreign language. Someone responded, the two men leaped up and ran past the trailer and toward the downhill side of the trail.

Bolan waited only a moment longer, then rushed over the twenty feet, through the brush and into the compound. Someone to his left screamed and fired. Bolan dived, brought up the Childers and blasted one round. The green-clad figure was twenty yards away but eight of the .33-caliber slugs caught him and spun him backward.

The Executioner turned to his right and charged toward the trailer. One man came around the far side, lifted a pistol and fired, then ducked away before Bolan could aim. Another soldier ran toward him from the downhill entrance. The Executioner darted behind the trailer and checked the area, then looked around the aluminum body again. Two troopers stormed toward him. One round from the Childers knocked both of them flat, but Bolan saw six more bringing up the rear.

Bolan never saw the man behind him. The first indication was when the M-16 on single shot barked and the slug drove into Bolan's left thigh and sliced on through. He dived forward, triggering one shot at the advancing men, then rolled. His attacker was working with a jammed weapon and before he could clear it, the Executioner blasted a round of double-ought buck into him.

Bolan saw a half-dozen more men streaming toward him. There was no choice. He had to check out his leg, then come in from a different angle. Now he was sure what was here and that he did not want to harm the trailer or any of its equipment. Sooner or later Dr. Dunning was going to have to give those MIRVs back to their respective governments.

The Executioner started to backtrack, limping only a little. He knew he was losing blood, but he could not tell how much yet. One man to the left fired and Bolan sent two rounds of double-ought buck after him. Then Bolan plunged into the thickest of the underbrush and worked silently away from the scene. He could hear them following him. For half a mile he jogged away from them until he found a thicket of wild briars and brush and gently wormed his way into it. He was concealed and they would not bother to look inside.

Gingerly he examined his leg. The wound had not slowed him more than half a step, but he had lost blood. Quickly Bolan pulled a bandage from his first-aid kit on his belt and wrapped the twin wounds on each side to stop the bleeding. Then he waited.

They came, but were a hundred yards to the left. No one approached the thicket.

They gave up at dark and faded away. Bolan had taken the time to catch a few hours' patrol sleep, that state of total relaxation and mind rest, but with all vital senses on alert. Now he stood, felt the stiffness in his leg and slowly worked his way out of the thicket. He had to get to their emergency assembly point to see if Kitty was there.

He had not planned on her getting hurt or captured, but he would not cry bitter tears if she did. The tall pine with the twisted top was harder to find at night, but Bolan got there an hour later. Kitty sat at the base, sleeping. He roused her gently and her hand flew to her weapon.

"Easy, easy, it's Mack."

"What happened? I thought we were going to capture the place."

"We probed it, and now we know more about them. Did you get hurt?"

"Just a scratch."

"Let's see it."

The round had gone in her shoulder and left a bloody wound and had not come out. She could still move her arm and did not seem to be in too much pain.

"You still on the team?"

"Yes. How is your leg?"

"Just a scratch."

"But of course. Do we go back in tonight?"

"I work best at night. Can you walk?" She nodded. "Good, let's move. This time we hit them from the other side, away from the trailer. But we go in silently. By morning we'll have their ranks cut down to size."

"Nothing new on the radio. The big powers are gathering the diamonds. One commentator said the two hundred million was about what one missile full of MIRV warheads cost. So it is a cheap solution to the problem."

"We'd better get moving. Thank your Russian ancestors there isn't a moon tonight." He paused. "Now we'll see how good you are. The real test of a combat soldier comes in the dark."

17

The Executioner and his KGB helper walked quickly through the trees toward the far side of the target, midway between where Bolan had hit them and where Kitty had struck. They were still a quarter of a mile away when Bolan realized the game had changed. Ahead he could see a glow of lights. Yamaguchi had planned with night in mind. As they came up slowly they learned the bad news.

The entire perimeter of the small armed camp was lighted up. Bolan wished he had a long gun to knock out the lamps. He would have to go in and blast the lights with double-ought buck, and that put him in too damn close.

Bolan had considered blowing up the generator, launching a silent attack against it, but then realized he couldn't. That would eliminate all the electrical power to the facility, and there would be no way to send the MIRVs back to their proper owners.

It would have to be stealth and finesse.

The Executioner and his companion moved the final twenty yards and looked down on the encampment. It seemed the same, except for the lights. The trailer door was open, the tall steps still there for access, and men walked around with submachine guns slung over their shoulders. A cooking fire and open-air mess had been set up under some trees where an overhead shelter had been stretched.

The Executioner grunted as pain streaked up his wounded thigh. He thought about his next moves carefully.

A born combat expert does not have to sit and reason out his strategy. He is already equipped with the combination of thought, logic and reason, and the next step is simply there waiting at his command. Mack Bolan was such a soldier. Now he knew what he had to do.

"Kitty, I want covering fire. Find a secure position between two trees or behind a log, and give me automatic fire at any specific spot where I need it. Count your rounds. Keep them busy wherever I am. If they come out after you, don't be a hero—do a tactical withdrawal and keep as many of the guns busy as you can."

"Where will you be?"

"Busy. You'll see me now and then and hear me. I'll be using the shotgun. Before that it may be rather quiet. If you hear nothing for fifteen minutes, start some general covering fire into the far side. But don't hit the trailer. Dr. Dunning has to be alive to send that MIRV back to Russian control."

"Good luck. I was never efficient at that sort of thing—the silent kill."

Bolan left, bringing the Childers battle shotgun from his back, checking to make sure it was fully loaded. It was. He had spares in a pouch on his hip. He slid the weapon back in place, leaving his hands free. The Ingram still swung from the cord around his neck, but now he had secured it in his belt so it would not get in the way. He touched the pouches on his web belt. They were ready.

It reminded him too much of Nam: the darkness, the forest, the attack on an armed camp. For a moment the memories flooded through him: the death, the heat, the constant wet jungle, the luxuriant growth. Then he was past it and moving toward another enemy. Now he had to get control of the trailer.

He had no reading on Yamaguchi. The man had no trouble rounding up troops who would fight and die for him. The money was part of it, but men think before putting their lives on the line for a few thousand dollars, even for a hundred thousand, especially when there is a chance they will not live to spend the money.

The Executioner crouched in the darkness and searched the floodlighted area behind. From time to time he saw armed guards walking set positions. He timed them. No pattern, a random movement. Less than fifty yards away, the door of the control room trailer sat invitingly open.

Bolan smelled diesel fuel. He looked closer to his left and behind a wall of pine boughs found the light green Kenworth tractor. It would do for a start. He slid in that direction, and saw that the truck was just outside the lights. He put half a block of C-4 plastic explosive under the dash and attached a small radio-controlled detonator.

Fifty feet ahead, Bolan saw the first foxhole. It was just out of the circle of light, an exterior first line of defense. The man in the hole was nervous, watching in front of him and on both sides, then looking into the lighted areas and back again.

The Executioner crawled along the forest floor past two trees and behind a log, then paused when he was a dozen feet from the lookout. As soon as he saw the forward observer turn and stare into the lighted area, Bolan was up and running hard for the hole. The big man carried a two-foot-long piece of piano wire in his hands. Both ends of the garrote had been welded into a stiff loop that had been encased in a tough hard rubber tube to protect the user's hands.

Bolan took another step and stormed into the shallow foxhole just as the guard turned back. The defender's light-saturated eyes could not adapt quickly enough, and he was blind for ten seconds after he looked back. Those ten seconds were fatal.

Bolan's rush carried him into the small hole, straight toward the unsuspecting guard. The Executioner rammed the guard against the far wall. The big attacker's knees crashed into the enemy's chest, slamming his head against the earth wall. Before he could cry out, the deadly strand of steel looped around his neck and Bolan jerked the handle ends in opposite directions. The wire bit into the soft neck tissue, slicing through Adam's apple and voice box and a second later rupturing both carotid arteries. Thick red blood gushed from the tubes.

The Japanese man's face turned to Bolan in one last frantic effort to see who was killing him. Thirty seconds later his head drooped, and his arms fell limp to his sides from their wild tearing at Bolan's hands. The man died where he crouched, warm blood oozing from his ruptured neck.

Bolan dropped him into the hole, searched it and found two hand grenades, the old U.S. Army pineapple type, and a fully loaded M-16 with the grenade launcher mounted below the barrel. Five of the rifle grenades lay on a shelf cut into the dirt wall.

The Executioner grabbed the explosives, slung the weapon and continued to the left, working slowly. If there was one, there would be more. He found three others, eliminated each with the killer wire, and left half of a bar of C-4 in two of the holes with a radio-controlled detonator. One signal from a small radio transmitter in one of his pouches and all would explode at the same time.

Some distance ahead he found the Bronco hidden in the brush. He quietly lifted the hood and took out the distributor rotor. The car could not run without it, and Bolan might need transportation soon.

The harsh stuttering of submachine-gun fire rattled among the trees. Bolan ducked, then realized it came from Kitty and that it was aimed far from him. He was still not sure about her. She might try to blow up the trailer and Dr. Dunning and Yamaguchi with it, eliminating the threat, but he was not convinced that she would make her move yet. There were too many variables to consider.

Bolan slid around to the next piñon and scanned the lighted area. Men were diving for cover on the side away from the trailer. Good. The Executioner had considered the attack plans and knew that the ideal would be to waste Yamaguchi.

With him gone the hijack would fade away, and Bolan could deal with Dr. Dunning. But the wily Oriental had not shown himself. Bolan saw six men forming a unit, working slowly toward Kitty's firing position. He unslung the M-16 and dropped two rifle grenades among the formation, knocking down all six men. Only two got up to continue the attack. They were soon out of his sight.

Fire and move. Bolan sprinted twenty yards from the spot where he had fired the two explosives and a moment later return fire chewed into the spot where he had been.

The probe just went hard.

HIGH OVER THE FIREFIGHT a tired and bleary-eyed pilot swung the U-2 on another cruise along the target line from Houston to San Francisco. He was looking for a pinprick in a massive dartboard. It was almost impossible. They should have had a definite triangulation by now. The tri-guys kept yelling something about dual transmissions and satellite bursts and secondary transmitters. It was all a crock and they knew it. So they dumped it on him.

Something blinked in a scope that displayed a visual of the landmass far below. Somebody had turned on one hell of a big yard light somewhere. He concentrated on the spot and shot thirty pictures, moving up as close as he could with his zoom lens. Whatever it was, he would know shortly.

He turned the little plane with the gliderlike wings and kept on the trail across the southwest United States.

IN NASA HEADQUARTERS in Houston they took a call from Secretary of Defense Jensen.

"What the hell do you mean, you can't triangulate this bastard? He's made a dozen transmissions."

"Yes, sir. We know that, sir. We're just as confused by it as you are. It's done with some new kind of modem downstream from the transmitter, so the entire message is shot out in a short burst that lasts only milliseconds. By the time our instruments pick up the damn thing it's finished and gone."

"I don't want excuses, I want results. I'm sitting here telling this to the President! Do you know how that makes me feel, how that makes all of us look? I want that asshole triangulated within an hour even if it is wrong. Do you read me, General? I want it done right now!"

The phone slammed down and the general in Houston winced.

"Get that bird on the horn, U2-11. We've got to produce some results and do it yesterday."

A full colonel scowled. "I take it the President chewed tail a little. This might help. We had a message from U2-11 three minutes ago. He says he spotted something unusual in Arizona. That's Arizona again, sir. He said one section in the unoccupied hills is lighted up like a circus."

"Forest fire?" the general asked.

"No sir, stationary lights, incandescent."

"Tell U2-11 that nobody in his right mind is going to light up the woods at night if he's trying to hide. Get his ass back into motion and find something. We all may be back on guard duty at the DB barracks before long if we don't produce some results for the President—like now!"

"Yes, sir, I'll tell him. Instead of landing him we'll aim him back along the line for another look. And get a new plane in the air to cover Arizona, watching for a triangulation. Haven't we got something that will plot a signal's heading automatically, without some human getting in the way? Let me call those electronic people again."

The commanding general of the Houston facility nodded, but swore softly under his breath. This headache was getting bigger all the time.

18

Attrition. That was the best strategy Bolan could work out for this sensitive situation. The man in the trailer still controlled enough warheads to destroy most of the major capitals in the world. Bolan could not take any action that might trigger such a response.

With Yamaguchi in charge, there was no telling what might happen.

The whole area was alive now. At least a dozen men were running around looking for a target. Bolan waited and watched from behind a small ponderosa. He brought up the Ingram, pushed it on automatic mode and looked around the tree. Ten yards ahead in the edge of the light a green-clad paramilitary lifted his rifle.

A 3-round burst from the Childers slammed into the man's chest. Then the Executioner darted forward to another pair of trees. There was no counterfire.

Someone barked an order and the men who had been charging around vanished. Probably into holes, Bolan decided. Now it would be harder.

The Executioner heard submachine-gun fire from his left. It sounded like Kitty's. Good, maybe she could help a little. He ran to the next tree, his attention focused on the edge of the light, until he spotted the foxhole. This one was better. No head showed. Bolan grabbed a grenade from his webbing, pulled out the safety pin and let the handle pop off. He counted two seconds, then tossed the bomb into the hole ten feet away.

It exploded on contact, sending a gush of smoke and sound straight up. Scratch one Yamaguchi warrior.

The Executioner waited and listened. For two minutes he heard nothing. He circled cautiously in the darkness around the lighted area.

To the far left a figure slowly emerged from a hole, then the man scurried into the vehicle. Bolan had no chance for a shot. The trailer was sacred ground in this battle, totally immune.

Ahead someone fired from the light toward the darkness. The rounds streaked harmlessly into the night, away from Bolan. About twenty yards from the trailer, Bolan looked again and saw a yawning trench. A moment later a head poked up. Bolan triggered the Childers combat shotgun and two rounds of double-ought buck whizzed just over the lip of the ditch. Four of the slugs tore through the gunner's face, dumping him lifeless in his ready-made grave.

Somewhere ahead a voice shouted in English.

"Hell, I didn't know I was getting into a goddamn war. I quit! I just want out! I'm putting down my rifle and taking a hike."

Bolan did not respond.

"Hey, goddammit! I surrender. Just don't shoot. You wouldn't shoot an unarmed man."

Movement—there! The Executioner watched as a man rolled over a mound of dirt and began crawling toward the darkness. He was a few feet from it when an M-16 chattered its deathsong. The man screamed, rolled over and died in the dirt.

When the sounds of the shots died, an angry voice yelled at the remaining defenders. The shouts were in

Japanese, and Bolan could not tell where they came from. The speech was short and evidently loaded with threats.

The MP-40 sang its deadly tune again. Kitty. The sound was followed by the blast of a hand grenade exploding.

Silently Bolan continued his rounds.

Somewhere metal clinked against metal. To the right, deeper in the darkness. Bolan held his breath, listening. Another hole.

Whispers in the gloom.

Bolan waited, tuned his eyes to the darkness. Soon he could make out some shadows. Two of them moved. They dumped something on the ground and vanished, moving away from the compound farther into the woods and downhill.

Deserters!

Bolan moved up to the hole as silently as a cat until he was six feet from the defensive point. But no one moved. Suddenly a sound to the left of the hole made him jerk the Childers around. Nothing. Probably some harmless nocturnal animal, he thought. But he was dealing with nocturnal animals. And these were larger—and deadly. The Executioner continued his advance on the suspect foxhole. When he peered over the side he found a form huddled on the bottom.

"Get out of there!" Bolan commanded in a gruff whisper. "Or I blow your head off!"

A kid no more than sixteen crawled from the hole. Even in the dark Bolan knew he was terrified. The young Japanese boy shivered, his teeth chattered. The Executioner thrust the muzzle of the Childers against the kid's chest.

"How many defenders does Yamaguchi have around

the trailer? And I want exact numbers or you'll never see the rising sun tomorrow.''

The youth trembled, looking at Bolan and nodded.

"He has twenty-five in his force. He calls it Yamaguchi's army.''

"How many around the trailer?''

"Eighteen. Some more down the road. Three with trucks. But I know that four have deserted.''

"Why didn't you go with your friends just now?''

"I...I...I got cold feet, I was so scared. They wouldn't let me go with them.''

"What's your excuse now?''

The youth looked up sharply to see if Bolan was joking. The muzzle of the weapon had eased from his chest and now the angry-looking gun was at the big man's side.

"I can just walk away?''

"After you answer some more questions. Is Dr. Dunning still alive in the trailer?''

"Yes, Yamaguchi needs him.''

"Yamaguchi had planned to take over the operation all along?''

"Yes, as soon as he knew Dr. Dunning was planning it.''

"Who shot the guy who tried to walk away?''

"Yamaguchi. He told us he'd kill any deserters.''

"Where are the next defensive holes?''

The boy pointed them out, and Bolan motioned him to slip into the woods. The Executioner wasn't worried that the youth might turn on him later. He had smelled the fear on the kid. From the hole in front of him Bolan found two more grenades. He hooked them onto his straps and moved forward.

A new sense of urgency drove him on. He knew that

Yamaguchi would not sit still and wait twenty-four hours now that someone was outside shooting up his site. Yamaguchi would force their hand. Demand quicker payment, make some big splash.

A loudspeaker fractured the mountain silence.

"Attention! Attention! This message is for those forces now attacking our installation. If there is any more offensive firing, any more grenading or explosions, I will take the strongest possible measures. I don't make idle threats. If there are more attacks on my installation or my people, I will drop a bomb on Washington, D.C. Some people don't believe what I tell them. I'll let Dr. Dunning tell you why they should. He will let you know what we just did!"

The next voice was soft, low, distracted. But the words were clear.

"Within the past half hour the world was warned that if the delivery of the diamonds was not speeded up, a missile with a thermonuclear warhead would be dropped near Wake Island in the Pacific Ocean. Five minutes ago one of the MIRV weapons was detonated at sea level a hundred miles west of Wake Island. I did this at the demand of the man you know as Mr. Richman."

The air was silent for a moment, and a gleeful voice came over the speakers.

"You see! You aren't messing around with some fly-by-night beginner here. I've got an army. So if there is any more firing, any more offensive action, I'll drop a bomb on the nation's capital."

As soon as Bolan heard the threat he unsnapped the pouch on his web belt and took out the small transmitter. When the last words had faded from the speaker, Bolan turned on the small switch and pressed the red button.

The woods erupted with three explosions that came so close together they billowed into one gigantic roaring, pounding thunderclap and a brilliant flash. The two foxholes expanded to five times their size, and the Kenworth tractor ripped into three huge pieces and spread chunks of metal over half an acre. Luckily there was no fire from the nearly empty diesel tanks when they ruptured.

It was two minutes before the echoes from the blast finally ended in the canyons and valleys around them.

Bolan stood beside a big ponderosa at the edge of the darkness as close as he could work his way toward the partly open door of the trailer.

"Yamaguchi. I'm calling your hand!" Bolan shouted. "You're bluffing and we both know it. Now is the time for some hard negotiations. You'll notice none of your people are firing at me. Most of them are dead and some of the others deserted your army. The rest are wounded or hiding, scared to death.

"Now, I'll give you a break. I'm not the law so I don't care about your little extortion scam here. You come out of the trailer and leave Dr. Dunning alive, and I'll let you go right on walking toward the nearest highway with some of your men. You stay in there and you'll die the hard way."

There were a few moments of quiet, then the loudspeaker came back on.

"Now I know *you* are bluffing. My men are waiting for a killing shot as I have trained them. You will be the one dead. Soldiers of Yamaguchi, get this fast-talking bastard! The diamonds are on the way. They will be here just as soon as the chopper can pick up the goods at the Phoenix airport and fly in here. We will take care of this fast talker and then share the two hundred million dollars. Get that bastard out there!"

Only silence greeted his appeal.

"I warned you, Yamaguchi. If there are any remnants of the great Yamaguchi army, you now have free passage out of the area. Don't worry about Yamaguchi and his threat to shoot you. I'll keep him pinned down inside the trailer. You have two minutes to clear the area, starting now!"

Gunshots came from inside the trailer, evidently aimed out the partly open rear door. Bolan put two rounds from the Childers into the side of the trailer near the rear door, and the firing inside stopped. The shotgun slugs would not penetrate the trailer enough to do damage, but they cowed Yamaguchi.

"You have a minute and a half, and time's running out. If you are wounded, throw your weapons out of the hole, away from your position, and wave a white cloth, handkerchief, anything. You'll be attended to at daylight."

There was no sound for a few seconds. Then a voice shouted a question from Bolan's right. It was in Japanese. A voice answered from his left.

"Go!" Bolan called. "Get out of here and stay alive. This wild scheme won't work, so get out while you can."

Bolan listened. There were whispers, movements. Then a voice called.

"We're going. Keep him pinned down inside, whoever you are."

"How many are leaving?" Bolan called.

"Six, maybe seven. We're leaving three wounded."

They left, shadows in the night, moving with combat caution from cover to cover until they were out of the glare of the lights and into the friendly darkness.

"You're all alone, Yamaguchi. It's your move."

"The same as planned. I'm walking out of here in two minutes to meet the helicopter on the road below. I'll be carrying a gallon can of gasoline, and I'll have a .45 automatic trained on Dr. Dunning. You so much as breathe on me and the old man dies.

"The President has given orders that Dr. Dunning is a national treasure and his life must be protected at all costs. That includes the two hundred million in diamonds that I'm getting. So back off, bastard. You try and sharpshoot me and my dying act will be to kill Dunning. There's no way you can win this one."

Bolan's strategy was settled.

"Kitty," the Executioner called, hoping she could hear him. "Let them go. Remember Dr. Dunning still has to get that Russian MIRV back. If he dies, your government has lost it. Nobody else could figure the codes Dunning used. Let them go."

From ten feet away came Kitty's answer.

"All right, American, but soon we must capture both of them. I have the good plan. Will you listen?"

Bolan ran over to her and nodded. "I always listen to good plans, but we have to do it on the move. We have to get to the road and the possible landing site first. I don't think Uncle Sam is going to bring in those diamonds unescorted."

19

In the Oval Office, the President of the United States sat and watched his telephone. He had been alternately relieved and terrified during the past forty-eight hours. Now he was not sure how he felt. He had sent all of his advisors except his Russian translator out of the office.

The takeover of the hijack site by some mercenary had at first delighted everyone. Then the demands became known and the authorities had pulled strings and made deals to get the diamonds and transport them to the Houston area as quickly as possible.

The President felt a continuing anger that all of his scientific minds and their latest equipment could not triangulate the radio signals that the hijackers had used. Getting a reading on it so quickly was nearly impossible, he was told at last. He had chewed tail for ten minutes, then ordered them to resolve the problem. Finding such signals had become a high-priority research project.

Mr. Richman's threat to kill Dr. Dunning had put them into high gear. Someone had at last realized that Dunning held the key to getting back the MIRVs the rebel had captured. He alone knew the code to communicate with the computers on board the space vehicles. They were pleased about the end of the threat to blow up all of the MIRVs but were now nervous about the death threat against the only man who could get back the one U.S. MIRV that had been hijacked.

Two hundred million dollars was nothing compared to the value of the hardware they had in space. But his strong secretary of defense had assured the President that they would trade the diamonds for Dr. Dunning. There simply would be no deal if the man called Richman would not give up Dr. Dunning.

The President had been specific. At no point was Richman to be allowed to have the diamonds with Dr. Dunning as his insurance.

The hijacker had asked for a lot: a long-range helicopter and safe passage to Mexico. Once he got the gems and into the air, he would be blown to bits by a dozen patrolling Air Force jets high overhead. The chopper pilot had been instructed to stay at one thousand feet and parachute from the bird at the first fly-by by an Air Force fighter.

It struck the President as being odd that the spotters could not pick up the Mogolion Rim area on their scanners. There was something about a hill lighted up like a Christmas tree, but somehow that got lost in the confusion.

When he got Dunning back he would have a conference with him and convince him that his talent was still needed in the government. Hell, they could create a special commission for him to work on whatever he wanted to. That would let them protect him and at the same time monitor what he was doing. There would be a mole inside his office, of course.

And once they had the scientist back they would also have a big bargaining chip with the Russian Premier. Then they could ask for a lot from the Soviets to get their MIRV missile back.

Wake Island. He would have to send a team into the area to test for radioactivity, make some money available for the island itself for constant observation and scientific evaluation of the effects of the bomb. It would not be easy, but he could handle it.

Getting Dr. Dunning back alive was the big key to this one. The President hoped Jensen could handle it. Damn, he sure as hell hoped so.

KITTY HAD NOT WANTED TO JOG through the woods to the forestry road that led them to the trailer site. But she had relented after some protests. The Executioner had outlined his plans as they ran. Bolan wondered what other plots she had. The woman had been too cooperative lately. Bolan guessed she had her own set of schemes that she was holding for the right moment.

Once Bolan heard that Uncle Sam was bringing the diamonds here to the mountain for the pickup, he knew Yamaguchi had made a big mistake. Given a delivery point, the military would have it well socked in with security people long before the meeting. That meant they might be there already. They could come in from Phoenix or military test ranges over by Yuma, or choppers from Alamogordo's White Sands Proving Grounds.

Time, that was the controlling factor. Would they have time enough to set up? A flyover and para drop would be simple and quickest, but they needed more.

Bolan and Kitty moved more slowly through the edge of the wooded section, leaving the roadway when it entered the open valley area where the helicopter would land. Bolan decided the gasoline Yamaguchi said he carried could be for a human torch threat as well as a signal flare to let the chopper pilot know exactly where to set down.

It was still dark, with hours yet until dawn.

At the center of the half-mile-long valley, Bolan stopped. He surveyed the area critically, but could see no evidence of anyone present. He was about to circle the meadow for a closer look when he heard it. At first he was not sure, then the faint rotor throb was unmistakable. It had to be a military chopper, with troops and backup, for pursuit if needed.

Bolan felt that it would be needed, but he wanted to be in the chase bird.

"Must be one of Yamaguchi's helicopters coming in to take him and the diamonds out. I'll try to capture it. You stay here and keep watch for Yamaguchi. My guess is he'll trade Dunning for the diamonds."

Bolan watched the dark silhouette of the chopper hovering at the far end of the meadow, as far away from the trailer as possible. Only one small probing light was on to let the pilot know how far he was from the ground. There had been no running lights, no strobes on the bird. Now he was sure it was a military aircraft. It was in combat mode.

Bolan started to move, trying for his usual running pace, but the pain in his leg now drove needles through the thigh and would not stop. He slowed to a jog and watched the pilot do a fine job of night landing. As soon as his wheels touched the meadow he shut it down. They had landed as near to the trees as possible, then two men jumped out and pushed the craft toward the pines.

By that time Bolan was close enough to hear them talking. Both were military.

"The other bird is only half an hour behind us. If we get away with the sound, this Mr. Richman shouldn't have any idea we're here."

The second man nodded, wiped sweat from his forehead and put a peaked cap back on. "I'll be ready when

I get your word. We're hoping on a one-shot mission. This little bird isn't equipped for a long chase."

Bolan watched the second man reach inside the chopper, take out something, wave and walk into the woods toward Bolan's position.

The Executioner slid from one tree to another until he was directly in front of the walker. The Childers came up, and Bolan stepped out from behind a piñon when the man was six feet away.

"Hold it! I've got a combat shotgun trained on you, but I'm friendly."

The man froze.

"Lay the long gun on the ground. Sit down and cross your legs, then lace your hands on top of your head."

The man did as directed. "How many tours of Nam did you have? I was there, too."

"I said I was a friend. You're here to waste Yamaguchi, also known as Mr. Richman?"

"One shot is all I need. Laser sighting. Seems almost like cheating. I blow away this Mr. Richman and we take Dr. Dunning back up the hill to get our MIRV back. Who the hell are you?"

"You won't have a chance to waste Yamaguchi, which is Mr. Richman's real name. He has a can of gasoline and a .45 in the scientist's gut. You kill one, you waste two."

"No way. I only do head shots."

"Ever heard of the spasm-reaction of fingers after killing head shots? You head shoot Yamaguchi and you waste two at once. So, we play by my rules."

"Kill me?"

"I told you I'm on your side, so don't try to be a hero. Your plan just won't play." Bolan knew it would not work to reason with this one. He brought the barrel of the Childers down across the sharpshooter's head hard enough to knock him out. The man fell into the weeds and pine mulch. Bolan tied him with line from a roll of forty-pound monofilament fishing line. Someone would find him later.

Bolan was nearly back to the center of the valley when he heard the second chopper coming in. There was no sign of Yamaguchi and Dunning. Then a hundred yards away in the middle of the meadow, a flame shot up, then lowered and remained steady. The burning gasoline was providing a convenient marker for the helicopter.

The chopper had full lights on and now swiveled stream lights toward the ground, picked out the two men and came down slowly fifty feet away. The backwash whipped at the gasoline flame, almost extinguishing it.

In the landing lights Bolan saw that Yamaguchi had Dunning covered with a pistol as they walked in tandem toward the chopper. As the aircraft's engine shut down, Yamaguchi screamed at the bird's pilot.

"Everyone out! I know there are three men on board. Send everyone out and then come out yourself. No tricks or you'll be a hearse with dead bodies to haul."

Two men ran from the chopper, and a third came out more slowly.

"Pilot, stand. You two, flat on the ground on your faces, arms over your heads."

Bolan ran silently through the grass, the Childers up and ready. The darkness masked his presence. But the same problem remained that he had told the marksman: there was no way to win with that .45 still jammed into Dr. Dunning's side. The Executioner would wait for an opening.

The pilot remained where he was but the other two dropped into the grass.

"Where in hell are the diamonds?"

"Inside, the way you instructed. I'm to fly you to Mexico," the pilot said. "You get the diamonds and safe passage into Mexico, and Dr. Dunning stays here. That's our deal. You agreed."

"Tough shit. I just changed the program. All three of us are going to Mexico. The old man is my only insurance. You know it and I know it and the President knows it. Come here."

The pilot walked toward Yamaguchi. Bolan could move no closer without giving away his position in the spill of the lights.

"Pilot, you walk behind me as we back into the chopper. You got that?"

"Yes, sir."

"Then do it!"

Bolan watched in growing despair as the trio moved into the helicopter, giving him no shot. At once the outer door swung shut, and Bolan knew the rig would be leaving with the diamonds and with Dr. Dunning.

He had to keep the chopper on the ground.

The engine rumbled to life, the whine began and Bolan raised the Childers automatic shotgun, aiming at the rear rotor area. He triggered a blast, then two more, but already the bird was starting to roll forward. He emptied the magazine into the rotor, but the bird had lifted out of effective range of the shotgun.

The two men on the ground were surprised by Bolan's firing, and started to stand up. "Stay down," Bolan yelled. "You'll be picked up later."

Then he ran toward the smaller helicopter, which was now moving toward him, skimming the grass. It set down and a moment later the door popped open and Bolan scrambled inside. He caught the surprise on the pilot's face.

"As you can tell, the hit didn't work. Now we've got to see how far that bird up there will fly with its tail-rotor assembly shot up. You better tell the Air Force not to fire on the chopper—Dr. Dunning is on board."

The pilot was storming after the bigger bird, which still had its navigation lights on. It was a quarter of a mile ahead, moving down the valley. Bolan quickly reloaded the 20-round, double-column Childers magazine and jammed it in place.

Five minutes later the pilot had gained on the bigger aircraft. He picked up his radio mike and spoke a cryptic three-word coded message. Then he turned to Bolan, a .38 revolver in his hand. He looked down at Bolan's hand and saw the Childers aimed at him.

"Hell, I'm no hero," the pilot said and put the .38 away. "Who are you and what happened to Sergeant Curtis?"

"The sergeant got tied up for a while, so I took over for him. If he'd gone in we would have had four corpses back there and no way to get back the MIRVs. I've been there, Captain. I've seen the look in a man's eye when killing becomes the most important thing in the world, no matter what side it hurts."

"What now?"

"Your contingency orders."

"Damn. If the chopper got off I was to shadow it and report its position for a knockdown."

"There won't be any splash this time. Your people should know that by now. So we follow Yamaguchi until he sets down somewhere."

"That might be quicker than we figured. That bird

ahead is losing altitude fast and she isn't stable. She's going in.''

''Can he set her down soft?'' Bolan asked.

''Depends how high he is over those trees and what you shot up in that tail rotor.''

''Stay with him. We've got to be there when it hits.''

20

The pilot of Bolan's helicopter stared below into the murky darkness at the navigation lights of the other bird.

"That chopper can't stay in the air long, not the way it's gyrating."

"Is that a clearing up ahead?" the Executioner asked.

"Could be. We'll know in a minute because that's where it's going to land or crash." Bolan's pilot increased his forward speed to maximum and slanted in, closing rapidly on the wildly swinging helicopter. It made forward progress and stabilized for a moment, then settled to the ground in a mountain clearing.

"Set down as close as you can get," Bolan shouted. The pilot nodded as he circled the chopper on the ground. Its landing gear was broken and the aircraft now leaned to one side. The rotor blade had barely cleared the ground.

"Let's go in," the pilot said, flying the bird into the grassland. He went into stationary hover two feet off the ground. Bolan jumped out before the wheels touched and ran for the stricken chopper. As he approached, a shot slashed past him and he dropped into the grass and rolled to his right.

Bolan thought he could hear someone talking in the big helicopter. Then the door burst open on the side closer to the ground and two forms came out. Here there was no light from a gasoline fire, only spill light from the downed aircraft.

"You out there. This is Yamaguchi. I'm taking over your bird. I don't care how many guns you have. I have what you want—Dr. Dunning. First, I need both of you to transfer these six boxes of diamonds into the other chopper. Any hesitation and I put a pair of .45 slugs through the old man here. Let's move it, you two. It's going to be daylight too damn quick."

"Yamaguchi," Bolan thundered at him, "where in hell did you get the idea the U.S. wants Dr. Dunning alive? I'm the Army sharpshooter they brought in to waste this dude. You'll be doing me a favor by blowing him away right now.

"Hell, Yamaguchi, we don't want your scientist friend. My pilot and me decided to go free-lance. We gonna team up and waste both of you, and the pilot, too, and take off with that two hundred million in uncut diamonds."

"No sale," Yamaguchi said. "I talked to the President. I know what he wants. Hell, you need this guy to get your pet MIRV back."

"Just told you, asshole, we ain't the U.S. government out here. We're on our own. Your scientist guy don't mean shit to us. We just want the diamonds. You understand now?"

The pilot of the downed bird came out the lighted doorway carrying a small cardboard box. As soon as he got twenty feet from the helicopter and well into the darkness, he dropped the box and ran, zigzagging for the closest patch of trees.

"There goes your work force, Yamaguchi. And the Air Force is on its way here now with gunships. They can blow you and your friend into a thousand pieces.

You ready to deal with us yet?'' Bolan lifted the Childers shotgun and sent two rounds into the end of the fuselage near the back rotor, the lead slugs shattering the thin metal.

When the sound of the firing stopped, the night silence closed around them.

Nothing.

Bolan waited two more minutes, then began working silently forward. It took him five minutes to cover the fifty feet to the stricken chopper. The lights were still on inside. The Executioner pressed his ear against the metal skin, and for a moment he thought he heard a soft groan. He dropped down and looked over the step plate on the door. Inside the canted helicopter he could see someone in the seat, his head thrown back. Bolan guessed it was Dunning.

Bolan lifted the Childers and surged through the door, his eyes sweeping the cabin and cockpit areas that he could not see before.

The kidnapper was not in the chopper. Bolan hurried to the scientist and studied the unconscious form. A finger test on Dunning's pulse showed a strong, steady heartbeat.

Satisfied the scientist was all right, Bolan looked around. Another cardboard box had broken open, spilling hundreds of the uncut diamonds on the floor.

He fingered some of the rough gems. Magnificent, and real. He picked up ten of the rough stones and put them in the shotgun shell pouch on his web belt. Then he shook his head and he pulled them out again, placing them in the container. He couldn't do it. He wouldn't do it. He'd continue to depend on people like Kurtzman, who could channel funds from the Stony Man cache.

Bolan jumped out the door into the darkness and ran back toward the other chopper. He found the pilot standing by the open door, holding a revolver.

"Yamaguchi's gone and Dunning is hurt. You can pick him up and the diamonds and take them back to the mountain meadow by the hijack trailer." Bolan said.

"Our Japanese friend is probably trying to circle around and get my bird. I'll stay right here, radio in the news and have some help come in. What about the other pilot?"

"He ran into the woods. After it gets light you can pick him up. Then come back and get me. First I want Yamaguchi's eyeballs served up on a platter."

"How will I find you if he's running?"

"Have a portable two-way?"

The pilot shook his head.

"No problem. I'll find him at daybreak. Then I'll start a big bonfire and send up a smoke signal. Just follow it and try to get there before the forest rangers. They'll raise all kinds of hell."

Dr. Dunning was moving and moaning, trying to sit up. Satisfied he'd be all right, the Executioner ran under the helicopter and headed for the woods. As soon as he gained cover in the trees he stopped and listened. Nothing.

Bolan settled down with his back to a tree. Without some audio input there was nothing he could do until morning. Then he would use his tracking skills, find the place where Yamaguchi had entered the woods and trail him. He had to remember the pilot was in the woods, too, but he would not move far from the clearing. And with dawn the flyer would run back to the chopper in the meadow.

Half an hour later a fighter plane streaked low over the valley, just skimming the treetops. It made three passes, then screamed off into the night. Another half hour and a huge chopper soared in, circled and snapped on its stream lights, turning the area into daylight.

It gradually settled down between the two birds.

Bolan had moved back to the fringe of the trees and saw six armed men sprint out the door of the big chopper. They ran toward the shot-up helicopter. Four more men with guns came out and formed the rest of the security ring around the three aircraft. Bolan settled down to wait.

AN HOUR LATER the first gray streaks of dawn lanced the quiet mountain meadow. Bolan immediately began searching the area for signs of passage. He found a trampled young pine tree, then ten feet ahead, a boot print in a gopher mound.

The line of travel seemed consistent: downhill and toward the end of the valley, which opened into another valley.

Like the night, Yamaguchi was on the run.

After a mile the Executioner was still finding signs of the hijacker's flight. Then Bolan thought he caught a whiff of smoke. He sniffed, looking around for a rise in the terrain. He spotted a small hill and made his way to the highest point where he could look right across the valley. His sense of smell had not betrayed him. Less than half a mile ahead he saw a thin column of light blue smoke spiraling up through the pines.

Yamaguchi must have started a fire to ward off the mountain chill. Bolan ran as fast as he could. His leg was stiff this morning, and the bandage was dirty and leaking blood. Only a minor inconvenience.

He came up silently on the smoke trail. It was in a heavily wooded ravine. The Executioner watched the area from above for a minute, but saw no movement. He darted silently from tree to tree until he could see the small fire. But no one was in sight. Bolan moved in as close as he dared without giving away his position. He scanned the area, looking for tracks or some indication of direction.

Then it hit him. It was a trap!

No sooner had the realization dawned on him when the deadly sound of a gun being cocked came from behind. He started to turn.

"You fell for it. Don't move, sucker. Not yet. But I do want to see who you are before I kill you. Now, hands over your head and turn around slowly."

The Executioner moved as directed and saw Yamaguchi's grinning face and flattop haircut. He was smaller than Bolan had expected.

"You lose," Bolan said.

"Uh-uh. This .45 is centered on your chest. Who the hell are you? Federal?"

"It doesn't matter. Winning and losing matter. And you lost your two hundred million in diamonds."

"But you lose your life."

"You didn't think I'd come out here without a backup. The pilot is over there with his M-16 trained on you right now."

"Bullshit. There ain't nobody. I've been watching you for five minutes."

"Suit yourself." Bolan saw the man's eyes flicker as a look of doubt crept across his features. The Executioner knew that Yamaguchi was itching to turn, but afraid to take the chance.

The Oriental scowled and tightened his grip on the

.45. Then, when Bolan thought he had given up on the idea, Yamaguchi shot a quick glance to the side. Bolan dived to the right as soon as Yamaguchi turned his head.

The Executioner heard the .45 roar and felt a jolt on his chest where the Ingram submachine gun was tied, but nothing more. Another slug whizzed by, but Bolan had rolled behind a huge fallen pine and out of sight.

He brought up the Childers and took a quick look over the log. The Japanese man had disappeared. Bolan crawled to the end of the twenty-foot log and looked again. From the new angle he could see Yamaguchi watching the other end of the fallen tree where Bolan had been moments before.

Bolan triggered six rounds from the body-shredder at the partly hidden figure. Bolan heard a scream of pain. As he watched, Yamaguchi shifted farther behind the tree.

Wounded? Or a bluff? Bolan stood and dashed to a thick ponderosa. He saw Yamaguchi dart to another tree, but there was no time for a shot.

"Give it up, Yamaguchi. Your army is dead or deserted. Your diamonds are gone and it's down to you and me. I figure you have two rounds left in that .45 and no spare magazines."

Bark over Bolan's head splintered as a .45 slug chewed into the tree. The Executioner ducked and peered around the other side.

"I have six more magazines, hotshot. But I'll need only one slug to send you to hell. Come get me."

Bolan checked the Ingram. It was useless. The .45 round had jammed the mechanism. But it had saved his life. He unslung the weapon and dropped it to the forest floor.

Then he raised the Childers to assault-fire position

and ran toward Yamaguchi, pumping a burst of double-ought buck at the man's hiding spot.

There was no return fire.

When Bolan got there he found that the Japanese had slipped away. The Executioner moved behind the pine and cautiously poked his head out, then behind him. As he listened, his trained ear picked up some slight sounds—crackling pine needles. Bolan moved that way, silently, the Childers ready. He gained the top of a rise in time to see a boot disappear behind a tree. Bolan did the same, then peered out from near the ground.

Yamaguchi looked to the rear, toward Bolan, then ran forward.

This time Bolan caught him in the open and saw that he was limping, favoring his right leg. The Executioner fired a round past Yamaguchi. The man stopped and turned slowly, the .45 held at his side.

The two warriors stared at each other.

Yamaguchi let the weapon fall to the ground. "You won't shoot an unarmed man."

"Bad bet," Bolan said and triggered the combat shotgun. The round jammed.

There was a desperate silence.

Yamaguchi screamed in anger, drew a six-inch hunting knife and rushed toward Bolan. The nightfighter only had time to pull the K-Bar knife and slip the jammed shotgun off his shoulder.

"I'll slice you into dog food!" Yamaguchi screamed.

Bolan held the K-Bar like a saber, the blade pointing outward in a classic fighting stance. He dodged the charging Oriental, the deadly swipe missing Bolan's knife arm by a fraction of an inch.

Seeing his enemy slightly off balance, Bolan kicked

out sharply with his right boot, driving leather into the man's thigh, pushing him backward.

Yamaguchi's glazed eyes bored into Bolan's.

"So, you fight dirty," the Oriental snarled. "I invented dirty!" He drove in hard again, slashing at Bolan's midriff. But the Executioner jumped back, avoiding the wicked steel.

Bolan then lunged forward, the K-Bar racing upward to Yamaguchi's chest. The man caught Bolan's wrist in an iron grip, stopping the lethal thrust. Then the Oriental saw an opening—Bolan's unprotected left side.

The hunting knife came stabbing down, but not fast enough. The Executioner blocked the maneuver, grasping Yamaguchi's knife arm.

The two men were inches from each other, locked in combat, sweat glistening on their faces, breaths steaming in the early morning air.

The Oriental's face was contorted into a deathlike mask as he tried desperately to overwhelm his opponent.

Neither of the two gladiators gave an inch. Then Bolan's knee sped upward, piston fast, ramming into Yamaguchi's crotch. The man fell to the ground, screaming in agony. But he still clutched the hunting knife.

Bolan used the opportunity to dive for the Childers. He released the magazine in the combat shotgun, repositioned the jammed round quickly and rammed the magazine into the weapon, charging it.

Yamaguchi saw the action and swung his arm forward. The blade came whistling through the air toward the Executioner. Bolan moved sideways even as the Childers roared, bucking in his grip.

Five rounds of double-ought buck shredded the Japanese man, pulping his face and turning his chest into a frothing mass of blood and exposed white ribs.

Bolan held the trigger back until the Childers ran dry.

The Executioner stared at the red, pulverized mass of flesh and bones on the ground, then turned and walked away.

The ravaged mountain woodland reverted to its stillness, just like a thousand years before.

Five minutes later Bolan found a clearing. He gathered some green pine branches and started a small fire. Soon a column of heavy smoke rose straight upward into the blue Arizona sky. Bolan sat down to wait, wondering how long it would take the chopper pilot to find him.

21

It was almost an hour later when Bolan saw the small helicopter circling the tower of smoke. The aircraft landed in a clearing at the edge of the woods. Bolan and the pilot carried the blanket-wrapped body of Yamaguchi and loaded it into the chopper.

"Figured the brass might want to see the corpse," Bolan said.

The pilot hesitated before he lifted off. "By the way, who are you? You aren't military, not in that black skinsuit. How do you fit in?"

"Just an interested citizen trying to do his part, that's all."

"Sure, with combat webbing, hand grenades and that shotgun like I've never seen before. A woman came out of the woods and said she was with you. She had a chatter gun with her. What the hell is going on?"

"My wife and I were up here camping, playing war games, and this guy and his army kept trying to kill us. Hell, we shot back with real rounds."

"You expect me to believe that?"

"Be damn glad if you do. I don't like a lot of questions."

The pilot shrugged. "Well, they'll believe anything we tell them. If it hadn't been for you, Dr. Dunning would have been dead and Yamaguchi would be in Mexico with the diamonds and we'd be permanently out one MIRV."

"Who do you work with?"

"Oh, the name is Leslie, special agent with the FBI assigned to the President." He paused. "They will want a name. The woman said your first name was Mack."

"Right, Mack Jones."

The pilot grinned. "Sounds okay to me."

They swung back over the mountain and soon settled in the valley below the trailer, but this time at the near end. Bolan could not believe how the peaceful meadow had changed. There were six large army choppers squatting on the grass. A field kitchen had been set up to one side, and sixty combat-equipped troopers were positioned in a defensive line.

A small tent had been set up to one side, for the commander of the operation, no doubt. They landed between two of the big green birds and Bolan wished he could just slip away unnoticed, but two men ran up as soon as they touched ground and opened the door.

"I'm supposed to take you to see General Zedicher right away," Leslie said. "Any problems?"

"Not as long as I'm not a prisoner and can keep my gear."

"No sweat. If anyone asks, I gave you the hardware." He shut down the bird. "Let's go get this over with. I really don't like generals."

The general was busy in his small, hot tent. He was pleased with the radio report of Yamaguchi's death, and it took only five minutes for Bolan to explain what had happened. He slid over the explanation why he and his wife were in the area. He said simply that Yamaguchi and his army had challenged them and refused to let them past and that had made Bolan mad.

"Hell, General. We heard on our radio what was going on and found out that this guy had something to do with it, so when he tried to get away, I had to try to stop him.''

Leslie corroborated the end game and when the general looked at Yamaguchi's body, he turned away in surprise, shook his head quickly, and dismissed Bolan and Leslie.

The pilot breathed a sigh of relief and relaxation. ''Always glad to get that part over. Now, Dr. Dunning was not in too good shape when we got to him. There was more than just a nasty bump on the head. He said he'd get the MIRVs back to their proper owners after he rested for a couple of hours. He slept the rest of the night after we brought him in. Your wife said she was a nurse and would sit up with him in case he needed anything.''

Bolan tensed. ''Why don't we go and see them now?''

''Uh-huh. They're right up there at the side of the valley. That tent under the trees.''

They walked to the tent and the sentry on duty nodded at Leslie and let them inside. The tent had an interior screen, two folding chairs and behind the screen, two cots. No one was in the tent.

Leslie's face flared with alarm. Bolan held a finger to his lips for quiet.

''What the hell?'' Leslie said.

Bolan took him to the back of the tent. ''My 'wife' is really a KGB agent. She must be trying to kidnap Dr. Dunning with his expertise about satellites and our missile defenses.'' Bolan's voice fell to a whisper. ''Let's talk normally and go out as if nothing has happened. Then we try to find them. She can't be far if he's in bad shape.''

''You must be CIA. Sure, whatever you say.''

They conversed in normal voices for a while and went

out saying goodbye to Dr. Dunning so the guard could hear them.

Outside Leslie spoke to the guard. "Dr. Dunning is going to take another nap. See that no one disturbs him for at least two hours. If the general yells, tell him I'll be glad to talk about the medical problems we could have here."

"Yes, sir, Mr. Leslie," the guard said.

The Executioner and the FBI agent wandered back to a smaller tent where Leslie stepped inside and came out with an M-16 and four magazines. He nodded toward the woods. They walked down the edge of the valley and stepped into the brush and trees. Bolan took the lead, then doubled back to the rear of the medical tent. He quickly found signs of passage. It looked as if someone was dragging something, perhaps a foot.

"Did Dr. Dunning have a stroke, anything like that? Could he walk?"

"Last time I saw him he could walk. Maybe he's putting up something of a struggle," Leslie said.

They moved through the trees. It was a simple trail to follow, which worried Bolan for more than one reason. They had angled away from the upward slope to the trailer. Instead, they worked around the side of the valley, moving a little deeper into the brush. At a more heavily timbered section, the trail turned uphill and went over the low ridge and started into the next small valley.

"What the hell is she doing?" Leslie asked.

Bolan shook his head. He had shifted the Childers shotgun to full auto and held it ready.

"She must have a contact out here or can call one in. She had a little radio, and I never thought to check it. The thing received standard bands, but right now I'm sure it was more than it appeared. Probably she can reach her shadow operative with the transceiver. She was on a high-level operation, so she must have back-up."

"Let's hope we can get there first," the FBI man said. "What are the odds?"

"How long has she been gone?"

"I talked with her three hours ago."

"Lots of luck," Bolan said.

They trailed faster. A half hour later they came to the bottom of the hill and swung along the side of a small, open valley.

Both men remained motionless, listening. Bolan pointed and they spread apart twenty yards, with the Executioner at the fringe of the trees around the pasturelike clearing. Slowly they worked forward, keeping each other in sight, moving by hand signals, crouching low when they stopped to listen.

Bolan heard a cough ahead. He waved to Leslie and mimicked the sound. They advanced. Forty yards farther along the fringes, the Executioner saw a man standing beside a tree looking in the same direction Bolan was moving. The Executioner hurried to a big tree that would hide him if the lookout turned this way.

Bolan waited thirty seconds, then looked around the base of the ponderosa where he squatted. The spotter could have been a hunter, except he carried a submachine gun and wore a determined expression. Bolan pulled the Childers up and stormed around the tree, the muzzle covering the guard who saw him coming too late to jerk up his weapon.

"Quiet!" the Executioner growled. "One sound and you get a belly full of double-ought buck!" The man was in his thirties, a veteran. He glared, but remained silent. "Put the chatter gun on the ground, quietly, then stretch out on your face, hands over your head." The man did as ordered.

Bolan knelt with his knee in the middle of the man's back. Leslie came up and covered them, his M-16 ready.

"Where are they?" the Executioner asked. The man did not respond. Bolan grabbed the lookout's hand and bent one finger back until the man groaned. "One more chance. Where are they? Another ten seconds and I'm going to break your finger. Then we'll go for another one."

"They're all up ahead about two hundred yards."

"Who and how many?"

"Three and the chopper. Pilot, the woman and a scientist. They're almost ready to leave."

"Who are you?"

"Local guide."

"KGB?"

"Hell, no. They hired me to find this valley, and that's all I know."

"Maybe." Bolan tied his hands behind his back with some of the monofilament fishing line and bound his ankles. "If you're telling the truth, somebody will be back to get you. Otherwise, you'll starve to death in about three weeks."

Bolan and the FBI man moved forward, spread again, alert, ready. Before they got there they heard an engine start.

Bolan knew it would take at least three minutes to get a cold chopper engine warmed up and ready. They both ran. The pain in Bolan's leg stabbed him with every stride, but he kept charging ahead. They both broke into the clearing to make better time, and saw the bird just over a small rise.

"Shoot for the tail assembly and the engines!" Bolan shouted. "We can't let them take off!"

They were still fifty yards away when the four-place chopper began to rise slowly.

Bolan closed the gap and lifted the shotgun. With the shot spread he would have to be closer to keep from killing everyone in the bird. He fired one just ahead of the Plexiglass bubble and saw two slugs star the glass.

Leslie used his M-16, powering two 4-round bursts into the main engine. Bolan ran faster. At thirty yards he fired again, aiming for the engine, hoping the spread was not as wide as he feared. He blasted three rounds without letting up the trigger. The chopper kept climbing.

Bolan held the weapon sideways and fired three rounds. The slugs bore into the main engine compartment. The M-16 sang its death song as Leslie emptied a magazine and changed to a new one.

The Executioner ran again, getting closer, holding the weapon more firmly this time, knowing where it was moving. He put six rounds into the chopper's main engine compartment and heard the engine stutter and then die. The big rotors slowed and came to a stop. The bird landed heavily on its skids.

Bolan kept running, saw that the door was not open and that there were no window areas for fields of fire. He slammed against the side of the chopper and leveled the scatter gun at the door.

"Open up!" Bolan bellowed. "We've got you zeroed in from three sides. Come out one at a time. If Dr. Dunning dies, the rest of you are turkey meat. Move it, now!"

Bolan slammed his open hand against the fuselage metal, and he saw the door unlatch. The panel swung outward and to Bolan's surprise, Dr. Dunning stepped out and held the door. There was no obvious disability Bolan could see.

"Gentlemen, thank you for your timely arrival. I kept telling them I hadn't even purchased a ticket for this flight."

A long, shapely leg came out of the doorway, then the rest of Kitty. She was wrapping a bandage around her left arm.

"Kitty, what a surprise!" the Executioner said.

"Bastard! No shotgun can fire that many times."

"I see it nicked you. Where's the pilot?"

"Dead. Your rounds also nicked him. I had to push Dr. Dunning to the floor."

"Thanks. You just saved yourself one MIRV in outer space. Now drop the purse."

She did.

Leslie came up cautiously, went through the chopper door, then came out a minute later.

"He bought the farm, Mack. No way this bird will fly again. Looks like it's walk time."

"No way. Rest time. Everybody under the trees. Then you can use that radio in your pocket and call in friendly air." Bolan looked at the scientist. "Dr. Dunning, are you okay? You did a fine job of marking a trail for us to follow. How did you work that?"

The man who knew more about U.S. missiles and missile use and defense than any man alive chuckled. "Quite simple, really. I faked a small stroke, claiming my right side didn't work. They all bought it. I wanted some time to sort this out."

"Had enough time, Dr. Dunning?" Leslie asked.

"Good Lord, yes! When I knew for sure this attractive woman was KGB, that made up my mind. We'll make them pay a high price to get their MIRV back. I hope to confer with the President shortly. I think I can convince him to take all of our MIRVs out of the heavens. That was my only purpose in the first place. I'm not sure that I've even broken any laws.

"I can negotiate that with the President. I see no hurry in turning the keys to the access codes back to the governments. No rush at all. And I'll bet the President will agree with me."

Leslie cleared his throat. "Mack, it's time I called in."

"I figured you would. One request. The little lady and I have something to settle—an old appointment you might say. Unfinished business."

"Five minutes, while I talk to the general."

Bolan nodded, took Kitty by the arm and walked her down the edge of the timber where they sat on a downed log.

"You lose, KGB. I win."

"It seems so. You will turn me over to the FBI?"

"It's Leslie's bust. He helped stop you. Let him have the credit."

"Generous of you. I do have something to tell you. I have been halfway in love with you since we met. Perhaps I have lived here too long. Ten years now. Maybe we could make that halfway affair into an all-the-way one once more." She leaned toward him, her eyes closed, her lips slightly open.

Bolan lifted his brows, leaned toward her and caught the motion of her right hand. It darted to her open-neck blouse faster than he thought possible and came away with a three-inch knife, which she jammed toward his chest, lunging forward with all her weight behind it.

His one brief glimpse of her snaking hand gave him

time to move to the left and roll off the log. She leaped toward him, the knife tracking for his heart.

The M-16 chattered six times and five of the slugs caught Kitty in the chest, throwing her over the log into the grass. Bolan looked up at the FBI agent who held the rifle. Then the Executioner jumped over the log and knelt beside her.

Kitty was still alive. He held her head in his lap. No one dying should be alone. Her eyes flickered, came open.

"Just a scratch," she said, her voice husky.

"Of course. Better luck next time."

"No next time for me." She coughed and red smeared her lips and cheek. "I really did love you there at the end. You are the best I've ever seen. You should have been on our side."

She coughed again and trembled. Watching him, she continued, "It was a good fight all the way. Somehow I knew it would end this way. Only I thought you would pull the trigger."

She shuddered and cried out in agony, then the spasm of pain passed and she smiled.

Soon the pain was more than she could stand. Her head rolled in his lap and her eyes blinked open for the last time.

The Executioner looked up at Leslie. The FBI man walked closer.

"It wasn't your fault, Mack Jones. She was dead from the moment I knew she was KGB. When she tried for you with the knife, she just gave me an easy excuse. Want to take a ride?"

"No. Tell them I got lost in the big shootout. It's a nice day. I think I'll walk. If I go back with you there'll be too many questions."

"I figured. I know you aren't CIA. I checked. I don't know who you are, but I'm damn glad you were here." Leslie waited a minute. "Anything I can do for you?"

Bolan shook his head, looked once more at Kitty, now so white and growing cold, just the way April Rose had. Everyone looked the same dead. He turned and walked away across the meadow, away from it all.

EPILOGUE

Nearly two thousand miles west of Washington, Mack Bolan leaned back in a wooden chair against the porch wall of a general store. He looked at a pair of elderly men already in position and handed each a bottle of Pepsi Cola.

"Morning," Bolan said.

The men exchanged suspicious glances.

"You're late for the third time this week," one said, tipping the soft drink.

"Damn. Hope you ain't gonna run off at the mouth the way you been doing," the other old man said with a sly smile.

"Nope," Bolan said. He sipped the cola, tipped the San Diego Chargers football cap down over his eyes and relaxed.

This one was finished. After Kitty died he had walked back to his rental car and stowed his weapons in the trunk. For a day he sat in the mountains and treated his shot-up leg with antibiotics. He dressed the wound again, and saw it begin to heal. Then he drove into Clints Well, sat in the sun outside the general store, and every day since had bought the old men colas.

The old-timer nearest Bolan winked at his cohort.

"Say, stranger, you think it's gonna rain any more this month and what for if it does? You reckon the rain will hurt the rhubarb?"

"Nope," the Executioner said, without opening his eyes.

"Lord a'mighty. I knew it. There he goes again, just talking his fool head off like we didn't have nothing else to do but sit here and listen to him carry on. I tell you it shore ain't like it used to be. I mean, a man had to earn his right to sit in these chairs. Now just any shoot-off-the-mouth who wants to can come in and sit and talk your leg off. I had me a guy who come by here last summer. City feller he was, and he got to talking and there just warn't no stopping him. I told him...."

The Executioner relaxed totally. He nodded, listening to the old men talk. Then his chin fell to his chest and he slept, at peace for a short time, an extremely short time.

The Turning Point

It seems aeons ago now, yet I can recall vividly the total upheaval of emotions that pervaded my world when I first learned of the deaths of my parents and sister, and the critical condition of my younger brother.

So many gray areas have been clarified now in my mind that I feel compelled to chronicle these thoughts.

I pleaded with the base-camp chaplain to tell me the details surrounding my family's tragedy. Why my family? Why me? These questions echoed through my mind. But I knew the clergyman would not have any answers for me.

"Listen, my son. These are the questions that are never answered. Any attempt at an explanation on my part would be trite. Dare I suggest fate? Their time had come? I really don't know.

"What I do know is that this event is part of the master plan of your life. So I would implore you to try and understand that it's not so much an issue of the tragedy as much as the inextricability of your future with their past. Because I do believe that the path of your life has been clearly demarcated. I feel that you have been given control of your destiny."

I left the cleric's tent, thinking that his words did not make a whole lot of sense for me. Nor did they diminish the unbearable sadness and loneliness that now bore down on me with crushing force.

That night I sat on my bunk, questioning my very existence and circumstances outside my control that had brought me to Vietnam. Was I fighting to make the world a better place for everyone, indeed, for my family? God knows they never had too much in their sorry lives. Perhaps only love. And somehow in those hard times, love was just not enough. Would that I were there to keep them from harm.

I rummaged through my Army trunk and found the letters from my sister, Cindy. As I fingered the correspondence, I tried to picture Cindy's lovely face in my mind. But the image was as blurred as the words that swam before my eyes.

Cold dread clutched my gut as I tried to understand the powerful force that had choreographed the interplay of lives—mine and my family's—some 8,000 miles apart.

Did it mean that a nail was inexorably hammered into my relatives' coffins each time I squeezed the trigger of my rifle? Who directed that scenario? Was it God, or Satan? I would have no way of knowing until I returned home.

Those were the thoughts that assailed me then. They haunt me still, but in retrospect I feel free of any blame or guilt. Because today I understand the naivete of my ruminations in those dark hours. Just as I now understand the meaning behind the chaplain's words. My destiny is justice.

—*Mack Bolan*

JOIN FORCES WITH MACK BOLAN AND HIS NEW COMBAT TEAMS!

Mail this coupon today!